In the Absence of Angels

In the Absence of Angels

In the Absence of Angels

STORIES BY
Hortense Calisher

LITTLE, BROWN AND COMPANY

Boston   *Toronto*

*Published simultaneously in Canada
by Little, Brown & Company (Canada) Limited*

PRINTED IN THE UNITED STATES OF AMERICA

To Heaton

ACKNOWLEDGMENTS

Of the stories in the book the following appeared originally in *The New Yorker:* "The Middle Drawer," "The Pool of Narcissus," "A Box of Ginger," "The Watchers," "In Greenwich There Are Many Gravelled Walks," "Old Stock" and "In the Absence of Angels" (in a slightly different form). The author is grateful to *The New Yorker* for permission to reprint.

The author also wishes to thank the *New American Mercury* for permission to reprint "Heartburn"; *Harper's Magazine* for "One of the Chosen" and for "Night Riders of Northville"; *Harper's Bazaar* for "Point of Departure"; *Mademoiselle* for "A Wreath for Miss Totten" and "The Woman Who Was Everybody."

Contents

In Greenwich There Are Many Gravelled Walks 3

Point of Departure 25

One of the Chosen 32

The Woman Who Was Everybody 45

Heartburn 63

A Wreath for Miss Totten 78

Letitia, Emeritus 93

Night Riders of Northville 108

In the Absence of Angels 127

A Box of Ginger 145

The Watchers 160

The Sound of Waiting 177

The Pool of Narcissus 201

Old Stock 211

The Middle Drawer 230

In the Absence of Angels

In the Absence of Angels

In Greenwich There Are Many Gravelled Walks

O<small>N</small> an afternoon in early August, Peter Birge, just returned
from driving his mother to the Greenwich sanitarium she had
to frequent at intervals, sat down heavily on a furbelowed
sofa in the small apartment he and she had shared ever since
his return from the Army a year ago. He was thinking that
his usually competent solitude had become more than he
could bear. He was a tall, well-built young man of about
twenty-three, with a pleasant face whose even, standardized
look was the effect of proper food, a good dentist, the best
schools, and a brush haircut. The heat, which bored steadily
into the room through a Venetian blind lowered over a half-
open window, made his white T shirt cling to his chest and
arms, which were still brown from a week's sailing in July
at a cousin's place on the Sound. The family of cousins, one
cut according to the pattern of a two-car-and-country-club
suburbia, had always looked with distaste on his precocious
childhood with his mother in the Village and, the few times
he had been farmed out to them during those early years, had

received his healthy normality with ill-concealed surprise, as if they had clearly expected to have to fatten up what they undoubtedly referred to in private as "poor Anne's boy." He had only gone there at all, this time, when it became certain that the money saved up for a summer abroad, where his Army stint had not sent him, would have to be spent on one of his mother's trips to Greenwich, leaving barely enough, as it was, for his next, and final, year at the School of Journalism. Half out of disheartenment over his collapsed summer, half to provide himself with a credible "out" for the too jovially pressing cousins at Rye, he had registered for some courses at the Columbia summer session. Now these were almost over, too, leaving a gap before the fall semester began. He had cut this morning's classes in order to drive his mother up to the place in Connecticut.

He stepped to the window and looked through the blind at the convertible parked below, on West Tenth Street. He ought to call the garage for the pickup man, or else, until he thought of someplace to go, he ought to hop down and put up the top. Otherwise, baking there in the hot sun, the car would be like a griddle when he went to use it, and the leather seats were cracking badly anyway.

It had been cool when he and his mother started, just after dawn that morning, and the air of the well-ordered countryside had had that almost speaking freshness of early day. With her head bound in a silk scarf and her chubby little chin tucked into the cardigan which he had buttoned on her without forcing her arms into the sleeves, his mother, peering up at him with the near-gaiety born of relief, had had the exhausted charm of a child who has just been

promised the thing for which it has nagged. Anyone looking
at the shingled hair, the feet in small brogues — anyone not
close enough to see how drawn and beakish her nose looked
in the middle of her little, round face, which never reddened
much with drink but at the worst times took on a sagging,
quilted whiteness — might have thought the two of them
were a couple, any couple, just off for a day in the country.
No one would have thought that only a few hours before,
some time after two, he had been awakened, pounded
straight up on his feet, by the sharp, familiar cry and then
the agonized susurrus of prattling that went on and on and
on, that was different from her everyday, artlessly confi-
dential prattle only in that now she could not stop, she
could not stop, *she could not stop,* and above the small,
working mouth with its eliding, spinning voice, the glazed
button eyes opened wider and wider, as if she were trying
to breathe through them. Later, after the triple bromide, the
warm bath, and the crooning, practiced soothing he administered so well, she had hiccuped into crying, then
into stillness at last, and had fallen asleep on his breast.
Later still, she had awakened him, for he must have fallen
asleep there in the big chair with her, and with the weak,
humiliated goodness which always followed these times
she had even tried to help him with the preparations
for the journey — preparations which, without a word
between them, they had set about at once. There'd been
no doubt, of course, that she would have to go. There
never was.

He left the window and sat down again in the big chair,
and smoked one cigarette after another. Actually, for a

drunkard — or an alcoholic, as people preferred to say these days — his mother was the least troublesome of any. He had thought of it while he packed the pairs of daintily kept shoes, the sweet-smelling blouses and froufrou underwear, the tiny, perfect dresses — of what a comfort it was that she had never grown raddled or blowzy. Years ago, she had perfected the routine within which she could feel safe for months at a time. It had gone on for longer than he could remember: from before the death of his father, a Swedish engineer, on the income of whose patents they had always been able to live fairly comfortably; probably even during her life with that other long-dead man, the painter whose model and mistress she had been in the years before she married his father. There would be the long, drugged sleep of the morning, then the unsteady hours when she manicured herself back into cleanliness and reality. Then, at about four or five in the afternoon, she and the dog (for there was always a dog) would make their short pilgrimage to the clubby, cozy little hangout where she would be a fixture until far into the morning, where she had been a fixture for the last twenty years.

Once, while he was at boarding school, she had made a supreme effort to get herself out of the routine — for his sake, no doubt — and he had returned at Easter to a new apartment, uptown, on Central Park West. All that this had resulted in was inordinate taxi fares and the repetitious nightmare evenings when she had gotten lost and he had found her, a small, untidy heap, in front of their old place. After a few months, they had moved back to the Village, to those few important blocks where she felt safe and known

and loved. For they all knew her there, or got to know her
— the aging painters, the newcomer poets, the omniscient
news hacks, the military spinsters who bred dogs, the
anomalous, sandalled young men. And they accepted
her, this dainty hanger-on who neither painted nor wrote
but hung their paintings on her walls, faithfully read
their parti-colored magazines, and knew them all — their
shibboleths, their feuds, the whole vocabulary of their
disintegration, and, in a mild, occasional manner, their
beds.

Even this, he could not remember not knowing. At ten,
he had been an expert compounder of remedies for hang-
over, and of an evening, standing sleepily in his pajamas to
be admired by the friends his mother sometimes brought
home, he could have predicted accurately whether the party
would end in a brawl or in a murmurous coupling in the
dark.

It was curious, he supposed now, stubbing out a final
cigarette, that he had never judged resentfully either his
mother or her world. By the accepted standards, his mother
had done her best; he had been well housed, well schooled,
even better loved than some of the familied boys he had
known. Wisely, too, she had kept out of his other life, so
that he had never had to be embarrassed there except once,
and this when he was grown, when she had visited his Army
camp. Watching her at a post party for visitors, poised there,
so chic, so distinctive, he had suddenly seen it begin: the
fear, the scare, then the compulsive talking, which always
started so innocently that only he would have noticed at first
— that warm, excited, buttery flow of harmless little lies

and pretensions which gathered its dreadful speed and content and ended then, after he had whipped her away, just as it had ended this morning.

On the way up this morning, he had been too clever to subject her to a restaurant, but at a drive-in place he was able to get her to take some coffee. How grateful they had both been for the coffee, she looking up at him, tremulous, her lips pecking at the cup, he blessing the coffee as it went down her! And afterward, as they flew onward, he could feel her straining like a homing pigeon toward their destination, toward the place where she felt safest of all, where she would gladly have stayed forever if she had just had enough money for it, if they would only let her stay. For there the pretty little woman and her dog — a poodle, this time — would be received like the honored guest that she was, so trusted and docile a guest, who asked only to hide there during the season of her discomfort, who was surely the least troublesome of them all.

He had no complaints, then, he assured himself as he sat on the burning front seat of the convertible trying to think of somewhere to go. It was just that while others of his age still shared a communal wonder at what life might hold, he had long since been solitary in his knowledge of what life was.

Up in a sky as honestly blue as a flag, an airplane droned smartly toward Jersey. Out at Rye, the younger crowd at the club would be commandeering the hot blue day, the sand, and the water, as if these were all extensions of themselves. They would use the evening this way, too, disappearing from the veranda after a dance, exploring each other's

rhythm-and-whiskey-whetted appetites in the backs of cars.
They all thought themselves a pretty sophisticated bunch,
the young men who had graduated not into a war but into
its hung-over peace, the young girls attending junior colleges
so modern that the deans had to spend all their time declar-
ing that their girls were being trained for the family and
the community. But when Peter looked close and saw how
academic their sophistication was, how their undamaged
eyes were still starry with expectancy, their lips still avidly
open for what life would surely bring, then he became en-
vious and awkward with them, like a guest at a party to
whose members he carried bad news he had no right to know,
no right to tell.

He turned on the ignition and let the humming motor
prod him into a decision. He would drop in at Robert Vielum's, where he had dropped in quite often until recently,
for the same reason that others stopped by at Vielum's —
because there was always likely to be somebody there. The
door of Robert's old-fashioned apartment, on Claremont
Avenue, almost always opened on a heartening jangle of
conversation and music, which meant that others had gathered there, too, to help themselves over the pauses so endemic
to university life — the life of the mind — and there were
usually several members of Robert's large acquaintance
among the sub-literary, quasi-artistic, who had strayed in,
ostensibly en route somewhere, and who lingered on hopefully on the chance that in each other's company they might
find out what that somewhere was.

Robert was a perennial taker of courses — one of those non-
matriculated students of indefinable age and income, some of

whom pursued, with monkish zeal and no apparent regard for time, this or that freakishly peripheral research project of their own conception, and others of whom, like Robert, seemed to derive a Ponce de León sustenance from the young. Robert himself, a large man of between forty and fifty, whose small features were somewhat cramped together in a wide face, never seemed bothered by his own lack of direction, implying rather that this was really the catholic approach of the "whole man," alongside of which the serious pursuit of a degree was somehow foolish, possibly vulgar. Rumor connected him with a rich Boston family that had remittanced him at least as far as New York, but he never spoke about himself, although he was extraordinarily alert to gossip. Whatever income he had he supplemented by renting his extra room to a series of young men students. The one opulence among his dun-colored, perhaps consciously Spartan effects was a really fine record-player, which he kept going at all hours with selections from his massive collection. Occasionally he annotated the music, or the advance-copy novel that lay on his table, with foreign-language tags drawn from the wide, if obscure, latitudes of his travels, and it was his magic talent for assuming that his young friends, too, had known, had experienced, that, more than anything, kept them enthralled.

"*Fabelhaft!* Isn't it?" he would say of the Mozart. "Remember how they did it that last time at Salzburg!" and they would all sit there, included, belonging, headily remembering the Salzburg to which they had never been. Or he would pick up the novel and lay it down again. "*La plume de mon oncle*, I'm afraid. *La plume de mon oncle Gide. Eheu*, poor

Gide!" — and they would each make note of the fact that one need not read that particular book, that even, possibly, it was no longer necessary to read Gide.

Peter parked the car and walked into the entrance of Robert's apartment house, smiling to himself, lightened by the prospect of company. After all, he had been weaned on the salon talk of such circles; these self-fancying little bohemias at least made him feel at home. And Robert was cleverer than most — it was amusing to watch him. For just as soon as his satellites thought themselves secure on the promontory of some "trend" he had pointed out to them, they would find that he had deserted them, had gone on to another trend, another eminence, from which he beckoned, cocksure and just faintly malicious. He harmed no one permanently. And if he concealed some skeleton of a weakness, some closeted Difference with the Authorities, he kept it decently interred.

As Peter stood in the dark, soiled hallway and rang the bell of Robert's apartment, he found himself as suddenly depressed again, unaccountably reminded of his mother. There were so many of them, and they affected you so, these charmers who, if they could not offer you the large strength, could still atone for the lack with so many small decencies. It was admirable, surely, the way they managed this. And surely, after all, they harmed no one.

Robert opened the door. "Why, hello — Why, hello, Peter!" He seemed surprised, almost relieved. "Greetings!" he added, in a voice whose boom was more in the manner than the substance. "Come in, Pietro, come in!" He wore white linen shorts, a zebra-striped beach shirt, and huaraches, in which he moved easily, leading the way down the dark hall of the apartment, past the two bedrooms, into the living room. All of the apartment was on a court, but on the top floor, so it received a medium, dingy light from above. The living room, long and pleasant, with an old white mantel, a gas log, and many books, always came as a surprise after the rest of the place, and at any time of day Robert kept a few lamps lit, which rouged the room with an evening excitement.

As they entered, Robert reached over in passing and turned on the record-player. Music filled the room, muted but insistent, as if he wanted it to patch up some lull he had left behind. Two young men sat in front of the dead gas log. Between them was a table littered with maps, an open atlas, travel folders, glass beer steins. Vince, the current roomer, had his head on his clenched fists. The other man, a stranger, indolently raised a dark, handsome head as they entered.

"Vince!" Robert spoke sharply. "You know Peter Birge. And this is Mario Osti. Peter Birge."

The dark young man nodded and smiled, lounging in his chair. Vince nodded. His red-rimmed eyes looked beyond Peter into some distance he seemed to prefer.

"God, isn't it but hot!" Robert said. "I'll get you a beer." He bent over Mario with an inquiring look, a caressing hand on the empty glass in front of him.

Mario stretched back on the chair, smiled upward at Robert, and shook his head sleepily. "Only makes me hotter." He yawned, spread his arms languorously, and let them fall. He had the animal self-possession of the very handsome; it was almost a shock to hear him speak.

Robert bustled off to the kitchen.

"Robert!" Vince called, in his light, pouting voice. "Get me a drink. Not a beer. A drink." He scratched at the blond stubble on his cheek with a nervous, pointed nail. On his round head and retroussé face, the stubble produced the illusion of a desiccated baby, until, looking closer, one imagined that he might never have been one, but might have been spawned at the age he was, to mummify perhaps but not to grow. He wore white shorts exactly like Robert's, and his blue-and-white striped shirt was a smaller version of Robert's brown-and-white, so that the two of them made an ensemble, like the twin outfits the children wore on the beach at Rye.

"You know I don't keep whiskey here." Robert held three steins deftly balanced, his heavy hips neatly avoiding the small tables which scattered the room. "You've had enough, wherever you got it." It was true, Peter remembered, that Robert was fonder of drinks with a flutter of ceremony about them — *café brûlé* perhaps, or, in the spring, a *Maibowle*, over which he could chant the triumphant details of his pursuit of the necessary woodruff. But actually one tippled here on the exhilarating effect of wearing one's newest façade, in the fit company of others similarly attired.

Peter picked up his stein. "You and Vince all set for Morocco, I gather."

"Morocco?" Robert took a long pull at his beer. "No. No, that's been changed. I forgot you hadn't been around. Mario's been brushing up my Italian. He and I are off for Rome the day after tomorrow."

The last record on the changer ended in an archaic battery

of horns. In the silence while Robert slid on a new batch of records, Peter heard Vince's nail scrape, scrape along his cheek. Still leaning back, Mario shaped smoke with his lips. Large and facilely drawn, they looked, more than anything, accessible — to a stream of smoke, of food, to another mouth, to any plum that might drop.

"You going to study over there?" Peter said to him.

"Paint." Mario shaped and let drift another corolla of smoke.

"No," Robert said, clicking on the record arm. "I'm afraid Africa's démodé." A harpsichord began to play, its dwarf notes hollow and perfect. Robert raised his voice a shade above the music. "Full of fashion photographers. And little come-lately writers." He sucked in his cheeks and made a face. "Trying out their passions under the beeg, bad sun."

"*Eheu,* poor Africa?" said Peter.

Robert laughed. Vince stared at him out of wizened eyes. Not drink, so much, after all, Peter decided, looking professionally at the mottled cherub face before he realized that he was comparing it with another face, but lately left. He looked away.

"Weren't you going over, Peter?" Robert leaned against the machine.

"Not this year." Carefully Peter kept out of his voice the knell the words made in his mind. In Greenwich, there were many gravelled walks, unshrubbed except for the nurses who dotted them, silent and attitudinized as trees. "Isn't that Landowska playing?"

"Hmm. Nice and cooling on a hot day. Or a fevered brow." Robert fiddled with the volume control. The music became louder, then lowered. "Vince wrote a poem about that once. About the Mozart, really, wasn't it, Vince? 'A lovely clock between ourselves and time.'" He enunciated daintily, pushing the words away from him with his tongue.

"Turn it off!" Vince stood up, his small fists clenched, hanging at his sides.

"No, let her finish." Robert turned deliberately and closed the lid of the machine, so that the faint hiss of the needle vanished from the frail, metronomic notes. He smiled. "What a time-obsessed crowd writers are. Now Mario doesn't have to bother with that dimension."

"Not unless I paint portraits," Mario said. His parted lips exposed his teeth, like some white, unexpected flint of intelligence.

"*Dolce far niente,*" Robert said softly. He repeated the phrase dreamily, so that half-known Italian words — "*loggia,*" the "Ponte Vecchio," the "Lungarno" — imprinted themselves one by one on Peter's mind, and he saw the two of them, Mario and Roberto now, already in the frayed-gold light of Florence, in the umber dusk of half-imagined towns.

A word, muffled, came out of Vince's throat. He lunged for the record-player. Robert seized his wrist and held it down on the lid. They were locked that way, staring at each other, when the doorbell rang.

"That must be Susan," Robert said. He released Vince and looked down, watching the blood return to his fingers, flexing his palm.

With a second choked sound, Vince flung out his fist in an awkward attempt at a punch. It grazed Robert's cheek, clawing downward. A thin line of red appeared on Robert's cheek. Fist to mouth, Vince stood a moment; then he rushed from the room. They heard the nearer bedroom door slam and the lock click. The bell rang again, a short, hesitant burr.

Robert clapped his hand to his cheek, shrugged, and left the room.

Mario got up out of his chair for the first time. "Aren't you going to ask who Susan is?"

"Should I?" Peter leaned away from the face bent confidentially near, curly with glee.

"His daughter," Mario whispered. "He said he was expecting his *daughter*. Can you imagine? *Robert!*"

Peter moved farther away from the mobile, pressing face and, standing at the window, studied the gritty details of the courtyard. A vertical line of lighted windows, each with a glimpse of stair, marked the hallways on each of the five floors. Most of the other windows were dim and closed, or opened just a few inches above their white ledges, and the yard was quiet. People would be away or out in the sun, or in their brighter front rooms dressing for dinner, all of them avoiding this dark shaft that connected the backs of their lives. Or, here and there, was there someone sitting in the fading light, someone lying on a bed with his face pressed to a pillow? The window a few feet to the right, around the corner of the court, must be the window of the room into which Vince had gone. There was no light in it.

Robert returned, a Kleenex held against his cheek. With him was a pretty, ruffle-headed girl in a navy-blue dress with a red arrow at each shoulder. He switched on another lamp. For the next arrival, Peter thought, surely he will tug back a velvet curtain or break out with a heraldic flourish of drums, recorded by Red Seal. Or perhaps the musty wardrobe was opening at last and was this the skeleton — this girl who had just shaken hands with Mario, and now extended her hand toward Peter, tentatively, timidly, as if she did not habitually shake hands but today would observe every custom she could.

"How do you do?"

"How do you do?" Peter said. The hand he held for a moment was small and childish, the nails unpainted, but the rest of her was very correct for the eye of the beholder, like the young models one sees in magazines, sitting or standing against a column, always in three-quarter view, so that the picture, the ensemble, will not be marred by the human glance. Mario took from her a red dressing case that she held in her free hand, bent to pick up a pair of white gloves that she had dropped, and returned them with an avid interest which overbalanced, like a waiter's gallantry. She sat down, brushing at the gloves.

"The train was awfully dusty — and crowded." She smiled tightly at Robert, looked hastily and obliquely at each of the other two, and bent over the gloves, brushing earnestly, stopping as if someone had said something, and, when no one did, brushing again.

"Well, well, well," Robert said. His manners, always good, were never so to the point of clichés, which would be for him what nervous *gaffes* were for other people. He coughed, rubbed his cheek with the back of his hand, looked at the hand, and stuffed the Kleenex into the pocket of his shorts. "How was camp?"

Mario's eyebrows went up. The girl was twenty, surely, Peter thought.

"All right," she said. She gave Robert the stiff smile again and looked down into her lap. "I like helping children. They can use it." Her hands folded on top of the gloves, then inched under and hid beneath them.

"Susan's been counselling at a camp which broke up early because of a polio scare," Robert said as he sat down. "She's going to use Vince's room while I'm away, until college opens."

"Oh — " She looked up at Peter. "Then you aren't Vince?"

"No. I just dropped in. I'm Peter Birge."

She gave him a neat nod of acknowledgment. "I'm glad, because I certainly wouldn't want to inconvenience — "

"Did you get hold of your mother in Reno?" Robert asked quickly.

"Not yet. But she couldn't break up her residence term anyway. And Arthur must have closed up the house here. The phone was disconnected."

"Arthur's Susan's stepfather," Robert explained with a little laugh. "Number three, I think. Or is it *four*, Sue?"

Without moving, she seemed to retreat, so that again there was nothing left for the observer except the girl against the column, any one of a dozen with the short, anonymous nose, the capped hair, the foot arched in the trim shoe, and half an iris glossed with an expertly aimed photoflood. "Three," she said. Then one of the hidden hands stole out from under the gloves, and she began to munch evenly on a fingernail.

"Heavens, you haven't still got that *habit!*" Robert said.

"What a heavy papa you make, Roberto," Mario said.

She flushed, and put the hand back in her lap, tucking the fingers under. She looked from Peter to Mario and back again. "Then you're not Vince," she said. "I didn't think you were."

The darkness increased around the lamps. Behind Peter, the court had become brisk with lights, windows sliding up, and the sound of taps running.

"Guess Vince fell asleep. I'd better get him up and send him on his way." Robert shrugged, and rose.

"Oh, don't! I wouldn't want to be an inconvenience," the girl said, with a polite terror which suggested she might often have been one.

"On the contrary." Robert spread his palms, with a smile, and walked down the hall. They heard him knocking on a door, then his indistinct voice.

In the triangular silence, Mario stepped past Peter and slid the window up softly. He leaned out to listen, peering sidewise at the window to the right. As he was pulling himself back in, he looked down. His hands stiffened on the ledge. Very slowly he pulled himself all the way in and stood up. Behind him a tin ventilator clattered inward and fell to the floor. In the shadowy lamplight his too classic face was like marble which moved numbly. He swayed a little, as if with vertigo.

"I'd better get out of here!"

They heard his heavy breath as he dashed from the room. The slam of the outer door blended with Robert's battering, louder now, on the door down the hall.

"What's down there?" She was beside Peter, otherwise he

could not have heard her. They took hands, like strangers met on a narrow footbridge or on one of those steep places where people cling together more for anchorage against their own impulse than for balance. Carefully they leaned out over the sill. Yes — it was down there, the shirt, zebra-striped, just decipherable on the merged shadow of the court-yard below.

Carefully, as if they were made of eggshell, as if by some guarded movement they could still rescue themselves from disaster, they drew back and straightened up. Robert, his face askew with the impossible question, was behind them.

After this, there was the hubbub — the ambulance from St. Luke's, the prowl car, the two detectives from the precinct station house, and finally the "super," a vague man with the grub pallor and shamble of those who live in basements. He pawed over the keys on the thong around his wrist and, after several tries, opened the bedroom door. It was a quiet, un-violent room with a tossed bed and an open window, with a stagy significance acquired only momentarily in the minds of those who gathered in a group at its door.

Much later, after midnight, Peter and Susan sat in the bald glare of an all-night restaurant. With hysterical eager-ness, Robert had gone on to the station house with the two detectives to register the salient facts, to help ferret out the relatives in Ohio, to arrange, in fact, anything that might still be arrangeable about Vince. Almost without notic-ing, he had acquiesced in Peter's proposal to look after Susan. Susan herself, after silently watching the gratuitous burbling of her father, as if it were a phenomenon she could neither believe nor leave, had followed Peter without comment. At

his suggestion, they had stopped off at the restaurant on their
way to her stepfather's house, for which she had a key.

"Thanks. I was starved." She leaned back and pushed at
the short bang of hair on her forehead.

"Hadn't you eaten at all?"

"Just those pasty sandwiches they sell on the train. There
wasn't any diner."

"Smoke?"

"I do, but I'm just too tired. I can get into a hotel all
right, don't you think? If I can't get in at Arthur's?"

"I know the manager of a small one near us," Peter said.
"But if you don't mind coming to my place, you can use
my mother's room for tonight. Or for as long as you need,
probably."

"What about your mother?"

"She's away. She'll be away for quite a while."

"Not in Reno, by any chance?" There was a roughness,
almost a coarseness, in her tone, like that in the overdone
camaraderie of the shy.

"No. My father died when I was eight. Why?"

"Oh, something in the way you spoke. And then you're so
competent. Does she work?"

"No. My father left something. Does yours?"

She stood up and picked up her bedraggled gloves. "No,"
she said, and her voice was suddenly distant and delicate
again. "She marries." She turned and walked out ahead of
him.

He paid, rushed out of the restaurant, and caught up with
her.

"Thought maybe you'd run out on me," he said.

She got in the car without answering.

They drove through the Park, toward the address in the East Seventies that she had given him. A weak smell of grass underlay the gas-blended air, but the Park seemed limp and worn, as if the strain of the day's effluvia had been too much for it. At the Seventy-second Street stop signal, the blank light of a street lamp invaded the car.

"Thought you might be feeling Mrs. Grundyish at my suggesting the apartment," Peter said.

"Mrs. Grundy wasn't around much when I grew up." The signal changed and they moved ahead.

They stopped in a street which had almost no lights along its smartly converted house fronts. This was one of the streets, still sequestered by money, whose houses came alive only under the accelerated, febrile glitter of winter and would dream through the gross summer days, their interiors deadened with muslin or stirred faintly with the subterranean clinkings of caretakers. No. 4 was dark.

"I would rather stay over at your place, if I have to," the girl said. Her voice was offhand and prim. "I hate hotels. We always stopped at them in between."

"Let's get out and see."

They stepped down into the areaway in front of the entrance, the car door banging hollowly behind them. She fumbled in her purse and took out a key, although it was already obvious that it would not be usable. In his childhood, he had often hung around in the areaways of old brownstones such as this had been. In the corners there had always been a soft, decaying smell, and the ironwork, bent and smeared, always hung loose and broken-toothed. The areaway of this house had been repaved with slippery flag; even in the humid night there was no smell. Black-tongued grillwork, with an oily shine and padlocked, secured the windows and the smooth door. Fastened on the grillwork in front of the door was the neat, square proclamation of a protection agency.

"You don't have a key for the padlocks, do you?"

"No." She stood on the curb, looking up at the house. "It was a nice room I had there. Nicest one I ever did have, really." She crossed to the car and got in.

He followed her over to the car and got in beside her. She had her head in her hands.

"Don't worry. We'll get in touch with somebody in the morning."

"I don't. I don't care about any of it, really." She sat up, her face averted. "My parents, or any of the people they tangle with." She wound the lever on the door slowly, then reversed it. "Robert, or my mother, or Arthur," she said, "although he was always pleasant enough. Even Vince — even if I'd known him."

"He was just a screwed-up kid. It could have been anybody's window."

"No." Suddenly she turned and faced him. "I should think it would be the best privilege there is, though. To care, I mean."

When he did not immediately reply, she gave him a little pat on the arm and sat back. "Excuse it, please. I guess I'm groggy." She turned around and put her head on the crook of her arm. Her words came faintly through it. "Wake me when we get there."

She was asleep by the time they reached his street. He parked the car as quietly as possible beneath his own windows. He himself had never felt more awake in his life. He could have sat there until morning with her sleep-secured beside him. He sat thinking of how different it would be at Rye, or anywhere, with her along, with someone along who was the same age. For they were the same age, whatever that was, whatever the age was of people like them. There was nothing he would be unable to tell her.

To the north, above the rooftops, the electric mauve of midtown blanked out any auguries in the sky, but he wasn't looking for anything like that. Tomorrow he would take her for a drive — whatever the weather. There were a lot of good roads around Greenwich.

Point of Departure

AFTERWARD, leaning their elbows on the mantel, they lit cigarettes and stared at each other warily. The late afternoon, seeping into the small apartment, pushed back its boundaries, melted them into shadow, intruding into the comfortably trivial box the long finger of space.

They were, she thought, like two people holding on to the opposite ends of a string, each anxious to let go first, or at least soon, without offending the other, yet each reluctant to drop the curling, lapsing bond between them. Always, afterward, there was the sense of a dialectic, a question not concluded; after the blind engulfment the two separate egos collected themselves painfully, slowly donned their bits of protective armor, and maneuvered once more for place.

It would be easy, good, she thought, to talk long and intimately afterward, to meet on close ground, divested of all pretense. But they never want this; they never do. The long, probing conversations that women tried to force upon them, getting closer to the nerve of personality — how they hated them, retreating from them brusquely into si-

lence, sheepishly into the commonplace of the consolatory
pat! Or, after the aura of wanting had ebbed, did they
too feel a little bereft, bare, in front of the speculative, now
disenchanted eyes opposite them; did they too conceal a
fumbling need to linger a little longer in the dark recesses
of emotion, to examine, to assess what had been separate,
had blended, and now was separate again?

Doubting this, she could see him, so quickly, so expertly
casual, leaving in a few minutes, gathering up his hat and
his brief case with a delicate assumption of reluctance, ex-
haling a last relieved whiff of tenderness into her ear. Out
of some obscure pride she never went to the door with him;
he never remarked on this but always closed the door very
gently, like someone leaving a sickroom. She could imagine
him standing on the doorstep downstairs, squaring his shoulders and making straight for a bar, eager to immerse himself quickly in the swapping masculine talk of baseball
scores and prize fights, blow by blow — all the vicarious
jaunty brag that sat upon him as inappropriately as a
cockaded paper party hat, but that was indulged in alike,
she knew, by the simple male and the clever.

Opposite, already a little absent, he stared at her a trifle
wryly, pulling gratefully at his cigarette. Now, he knew,
would begin the gentle process of disengagement that he
had learned long ago, defensively, to perform so well. Now
it would be like a game of gesture in which he excelled, in
which it would be as if, smiling the tolerant smile of experience, he divested himself one by one of a series of
clinging hands, until he stood again remote, inaccessible,
free. Only later, when the warmth and almost all the con-

quest had worn away, would the slow rise of irritation with self and women begin, then the slight guilt of satiety that would enable the resolve to be made, and finally the shrug and the forgetfulness.

Regretfully, as if taking leave of a landscape that had pleased, he broke his glance from the eyes opposite him, looked down at the hand that lay perhaps intentionally near his on the mantel, curved upward, open. Warned, he had felt all afternoon the too recognizable air of intensity, of special pleading, that had surrounded her; in a woman of less taste it would have taken the form of a dress too tight, or a flock of bows in the hair. Intelligent women stimulated rather than repelled him, if they had the other attraction too; their withdrawals and defenses were heightened by subtleties that it was a challenge to explore and subdue. But in the end it was all the same — gazing up at you afterward with their liquid pained stare, detecting the coil of softness in you that half appreciated, half understood, they all pleaded for an avowal — of what?

The hand on the mantel brushed his, and was withdrawn.

"It's pathetic, isn't it," she whispered, "the spectacle of people trying to reach one another? By any means. Everywhere." There was a rush, a grating of honesty, in her tone that she deprecated immediately with a quick covering smile.

The remark hung too nakedly on the air. He nodded ruefully, and allowing his hand to touch hers for a moment, he stared into their palms, and they stood together for a moment, joined over the body of their failure.

Patting her shoulder in a light rhythm, one, two, three, he grasped her chin tight in his hand and looked down at her for quite a time.

"See you," he said. "Better run for my train." As he took up his hat and brief case half embarrassedly, leaning against the mantel she was watching him silently, and it was so that he caught the last image of her as he let himself out the door, easing the knob to.

Blinking in the light of the outdoors, which was a lot stronger than one would suspect after that dim apartment of hers, he brought that image with him, but, shielding him, his mind shifted, rioting pleasurably among the warmer images of the early afternoon. All the way down the avenue from the park he carried these with him, until at Forty-second Street, sauntering toward Grand Central, he joined the streams of women carrying their light pastel packages of hose, ribbons, blouses — all the paraphernalia of women at the turn of a season. He was used to seeing them in the train, haggard after the day-long scavenger hunt for the hat to go with the shoes that went with the dress — riding home for the long ritual of unguents that would arm them once more. From his wife, and his sisters before her, he knew it well — the ritual that would transform the kimonoed, the oiled, the bepinned one into the handsome, curled, confident woman waiting at the door, Venus risen triumphant on a shell of empty boxes.

For a while now, out of a sense of the just, the cautious moment, he would be free, but inevitably he would be alert again to the puff of organdie at a throat, a mouth so richly, redly drawn over the scanter curve of lip beneath,

a look, plaintive or ripe — the whole froth of femininity
that they all put out like entangling scarves. They would be
drawn to him too, often out of an awareness of his sensi-
tivity to them, only to be confused by the proffered warmth
for warmth of a relationship that ended, not in the conventional brutalities of a rejection they might have understood, but in the firm, knowing refusal to be involved in
the abject spiritual surrender which they always ended up
by demanding, for which they all longed.

Either they caught you young and eager, as he had been,
and — nailed down by their allies, time and habit — in-
credibly, swiftly, you were a member of the country club,
with a mortgage, while across the room, herded together
with the others, in their unblushing, blatant discussions of
the idiosyncrasies of husbands, they proclaimed your inden-
ture to them — or else, in the byways of *sub rosa* relation-
ships, there too, sooner or later, they strangled calm with
their demoniacal need for finality, possession, grown all the
stronger because it could not be socially displayed. Perhaps,
he thought, it is the riddled period in which we live, in
which people are driven endlessly upon one another, hoping to find, in the person of another one of the bewildered,
the a priori love, the certainty, the touchstone.

He had reached Grand Central and the long sloping entrance to the suburban trains. Across the way his usual
stop-in place beckoned with its promise of a muted jumble
of light, noise, and clinking glassware in which feeling could
be drowned. Perhaps it is worse for the women, he thought,
but they *are* the worst — all of them Penelopes, trying to
weave you into the fabric of their lives, building on you in

one way or the other until you have to get out from under. Squaring his shoulders, he shifted his brief case, and walked on toward the sure nepenthe, the comfortable glaze of the bar.

In the apartment, she still stood at the mantel, reluctant to acknowledge the gap in the room, to close it over finally with movement, change. At last she walked over to the sofa and sat down, shrinking into the cushion for its warmth. The room was always like this afterward, like a deserted theatre, and, half actress, half spectator, she sat and mulled over what had gone before, forming, as if into a stylized ballet, the whole interchange of responses that had been their meeting, forestalling, by this means, the sure humming rise of depression.

Her last exclamation, which had been as alienating to him, she knew, as the shock of a cry for help thrust suddenly into the most casual of conversations, had come from the heart, the heart that she knew, by unspoken agreement with him, with all of them perhaps, must always be held behind one. Only among the very young might it be otherwise, possibly . . . before they had acquired the destroying talent for compromise that eased — as it more and more deflated — the drama of experience.

Perhaps, she thought, curvetting so lightly, so "modernly," as we have been taught to do, over the sharp stick of emotion, never daring the banal, the stark word, it is our reticences that trap us after all. It happened everywhere: behind the tidy doors of marriage, in the dark bed of adventure, or in the social bumpings against one another in the crowded rooms where people massed together protectively in frenetic gaiety, hiding stubbornly — "I am alone" — using liquor, music, sex, to say — "You, too?" It happened, sometimes, in rooms at the end of the day, after the scratch of gossip, the long political sighs, were done, and there was a lull, with people staring reflectively into their glasses, twirling the stems, that the lull deepened, a sentence died on the air, and it was as if everyone had plunged his arm into a deep well, searching, seeking — but no hands met and clasped.

She walked into the kitchen and poured herself a drink. Toward her through the window over the sink the stunted city trees stretched in the soft, mottled weather, all along their weak, cramped boughs, the sure, recrudescent leaves. It would be better if it were autumn now, she thought drearily, when people huddling together at concerts, at parties, in front of fires, can persuade themselves that they are huddled there together against the cold.

Tonight there were people coming in to talk. She knew beforehand how she would sit there, in the anodyne of company, cradling the warmth of what had been, while every so often, half savored because it gave a meaning to the hour, half pushed down lest it rise to the surface and become real hurt, there would come, like water washing over a sunken buoy, the little knell of sadness for something that had been, that had never quite been, that now had almost certainly ceased to be.

One of the Chosen

THE night before the fall reunion of his college class, Spanner had come home a little ashamed of his easy acceptance of the prodding special invitation over the phone that day from Banks, a man whose face he could not even remember. For years he had ignored the printed notices that came to him now and then, even though he lived in the city where the college was, but this time, Banks had said, there was to be a private conclave of all the members of the crew who had won the regatta for the college over twenty years before. Half reluctant to include himself in the picture of the old grads redundantly deploying the terrain of dead triumphs, he had found himself saying that he would come. He had been coxswain of that crew.

Thinking it over idly in bed later on, in those random images just before sleep, which carried with them unexpected prickings of realization that lay just below the surface of expressed thought, he had found himself dwelling, not on the members of the crew, but on all those odd ones, the campus characters who had existed, hardly acknowledged, on the penumbra of his own sunlit, multiform activities of those days. Why should he now think suddenly of De Jong, the spastic, who, jerking and shambling his way one day into the office of the college literary magazine of which he, Spanner, had been a staff member, had thrust upon the group there a sheaf of manuscript, and gargling incomprehensibly, had left before their gauche heartiness could detain him? The sheaf had contained a group of poems clearly derivative from the unfashionable Housman, and therefore unusable, but marked by a discipline of language, a limpidity, almost a purity of organization — as if in them De Jong had tried to repudiate his disjointed idiot face, the coarse clayey skin, the wide slobbering mouth, thickened with effort. They had avoided discussing him, until Black, the psychology student, had remarked, with his clinician's air, "I saw him once in Phipps' lecture class, way at the top, you know, in one of those high gallery seats. My God — there he was — twitching away at some lecture of his own — oblivious!" One of the others had sniggered nervously. The talk had passed on, and later that year, because of a lack of copy, one of the poems had been printed after all.

He thought now, with a belated guilt, of the grim separation that must have been De Jong's, and whether there would have been anything that the rest of them, if less swaddled with their own crude successes, could have done. He'd never heard the man mentioned again, or seen a reference to him in the alumni magazine.

Why now, in this context, should he remember George Shipley, the Negro basketball star of their era, certainly handsome enough, with straight, clipped features so completely lacking the prognathous bulges commonly associated with his race that this, no doubt, had had some effect on his acceptance on certain levels by the student body. Smiling, quiet, he had often sat near Spanner in the rotunda of the law library; Spanner had heard that he was a professor of law now in one of the good Southern colleges for Negroes. Why, burning now with something like shame, should he remember him at the dances to which he brought always the same prim-faced mulatto girl; why should he see him, wide shoulders bent in the *dégagé* dance fashion of that day, black features impassive, slowly circling with the girl, always in a small radius of their own?

Spanner was fully awake now and, raised up on his elbow, his eyes gradually following the familiar outlines of the furniture as they grew more perceptible in the darkness, he forced himself to probe in the archives of recall for others who, like Shipley, like De Jong, seemed bound together in his memory only by the mark of that rejection by the group, which now, in pitying retrospect, it seemed to him, had he then been less grossly unaware, less young, he, by some friendly overture, might have partially repaired.

There was the Burmese princeling who had lived at International House, who had treated a group of them to several awkwardly accepted dinners at Oriental restaurants of his choosing, whose foreignness and wealth had at first had a certain cachet, but from whom they had shortly retreated in ridicule, in gruff embarrassment at the hand, sliding as silk, the emotional waver of the voice. At that, they had never been sure that he was really . . . that it had not been just a form of Eastern cajolery, or a misbegotten sense of acceptance which had elicited the moist look, the overheated hand. Afterward, when they had met him on campus in a few curt scenes of misshapen talk in which it was evident that camaraderie had flown, his gestures had been restrained enough, Lord knows, his eyes sufficiently flat and dull, with reserve enough to satisfy the most conventional of them.

Of course, there had been that group of those others, pariahs without question, who convened always in that little Greek restaurant, the Cosmos, through the door of which they sometimes glanced out at you with the hauteur of tropical birds in a zoo, jangling consciously into conversation as you passed, with their tense, dulcet exuberance. Toleration of these had been more than one could expect of boys suffused with their own raw reactions to adulthood, which they covered up with a passionate adherence to the norm, with apprehensive jeerings at the un-average in its lightest forms, so that even displaying too good, too undulate a French accent, in class, was likely to incur for one the horse-laugh from behind. But could they have helped, with some small glow of receptivity, young Schwiller, that model young German from the cleanly swabbed villa in North Jersey, with too little money, background, or ability — too little of everything except a straining, unhumorous will to belong — who, after some covert, abortive incident on a group camping trip, had hanged himself to a tree?

Ah well, Spanner thought, fumbling in the dark for a cigarette, and lighting it in a thankful momentary absorption with the ordinary — these had been the extreme cases. But what of the others, less vividly obvious to memory because they had been more usual, or because they had perhaps already achieved their secret dikes of resignation? He remembered, for instance, all the little Jewish boys, with their overexpressive eyes, their thickets of hair whose Egyptian luxuriousness no barber could tame, and most revelatory of all, the forced vying, the self-conscious crackle of their conversation.

As a Jew himself, he had been helped, he knew, by his fair-skinned, freckled, almost "mick" exterior, by the generations of serene cosmopolitan living that were evident, implicit in the atmosphere of his family's sprawling apartment on the park, and frankly, he supposed, by the unrevealing name of Spanner, which his great-grandfather had brought over from England, and had come by honestly, as far as the family knew. His family had belonged among those lucky Jews, less rare than was commonly realized, who had scarcely felt the flick of injustice expressed socially, much less in any of its harsher forms. Still, despite this, it had been unusual, he knew, to remain so untouched, so free from apprehension of the lurking innuendo, the consciousness of schism — for in addition to his race, he had carried, too, that dark bruise of intellectuality, the bearers of which the group flings ever into the periphery, if it can.

That was where the luck he had had in being coxswain had come in. Because of it, although he had done well, almost brilliantly in his law classes, all his possibly troublesome differences had remained hidden, inconspicuous under the brash intimacy of the training session, under the hearty accolade of his name on the sporting page — because of it he had been hail fellow in the boat house and on the campus — he had been their gallant "little guy." So, he thought, he had ridden through it all in a trance of security which, he realized now, had been given only to the favored few, while all around them, if he and the others had not been so insensible of it, had been the hurts, the twistings, that might have been allayed. The image of the spastic crossed before him again, a distortion to the extreme of that singularity from which many others must have suffered less visibly, from which he himself had been accountably, blessedly safe. He lay back again, and turning, blotted his face against the dispassionate pillow and slept.

The next morning he awoke late. It was Saturday. Taking his coffee at the dining-room table deserted by his wife and children some hours before, he was half-annoyed at the emotionalism of the previous night. "Who the hell do I think I am — Tolstoy?" he thought, wincing. Rejecting the unwonted self-analysis that had preceded sleep, he finished his coffee offhandedly, master of himself once more. He got the car out of the garage and swung slowly down the parkway, thinking that if he delayed his arrival until well after twelve he would miss the worst of the speechifying.

As he approached the college-dominated midtown neighborhood, idling the car slowly along, he passed some of the brownstone houses, shoddier now with the indefinable sag of the rooming house, which had been the glossier fraternity houses of his day. He had heard that many of them, even the wealthier ones which had survived depression times, subsidized to plush draperies and pine paneling by some well-heeled brother, had gone down finally during the war years just past, when the college had become a training center for the Navy. Then, he supposed, those accelerated waves of young men passing through had not only not had time for such amenities, but, trapped together in a more urgent unity, had had no need for the more superficial paradings of Brotherhood.

Although he had had his fair share of indiscriminate rushing during his freshman year, he himself had had no particular desire to join a house, comfortably ensconced, as he had been, in his family's nearby home, already sated with the herded confinement of prep school. In his sophomore year, he remembered, after he had joined the magazine, and it was evident that he would have a place on the varsity crew, the best Jewish fraternity had been very pressing, then annoyed at his tepid refusal, and there had been overtures from one or two of the Christian fraternities whose social position was so solid that they could afford, now and then, to ignore the dividing lines in favor of a man whose campus prominence or money would add lustre to the house, but by this time he had already been focusing on his law career. Still, he thought now, he had always had the comfortable sense of acceptance; he had, for instance, never felt that deep racial unease with the Gentile to which his most apparently assimilated Jewish friends sometimes confessed. To be free from the tortuous doubt, the thin-skinned expectancy of slight — it had helped. He had been lucky.

In front of one of the brownstones not too far from Jefferson Hall, the old residence hall in one of whose rooms the luncheon was to be held, he found a place to park the car, and got out. He hadn't been near here in years; his life was a well-conducted bee-line from suburb to downtown office, and most of his associations were on the East Side anyway. He walked past the familiar architectural hodge-podge of the buildings, noting with pleasure that the rough red cobbles of the walks had been preserved, glancing with disapproval at the new library which had been begun in his time, on the field where they used to play tennis. Half utilitarian, but with reticent touches of bastard Greek on its lean, flat façade, it stretched out, two-dimensional and unassimilable, a compromise of tastes which had led to none. The vulgarization of taste in a place which should have been a repository of the best still had power to shock him; he was pleased at having retained this naïveté, this latent souvenir of youth. Around him and past him, male and female, hurrying or sauntering, or enthusiastically stand-ing still, was that year's crop of imperishable young, on their faces that which the college had not yet vulgarized — the look of horizons that were sure, boundaries that were limit-less — the look of the unreconciled.

Already, he twitted himself, he was developing the spots of the returning alumnus. The secret conviction that in-wardly, outer decay to the contrary, one had preserved a personal ebullience better than most, the benignant survey-ing glance with its flavor of *"si la jeunesse savait"* — he had them all. Smiling to himself he turned in at the doorway of Jefferson Hall, and making another turn to the reception room on the right, met the slightly worn facsimiles of his youth full on.

They were gathered around the mantel, most of them, talking in voices at once hearty and tentative, glasses in hand. Drinks to melt the integument of twenty years and

more — of course. From the group a man detached himself
to come forward and pump his hand.

"Davy! Why, Davy Spanner!" The lost face of Banks coa-
lesced at once in his recognition, fatally undistinguished, except for the insistent, hortatory manner that had battened
on the years. He had been business manager of the crew.

Banks conveyed him toward the others like a trophy.

"Look who's here!" he crowed. "Our little coxie!"

Grinning a little stiffly, Spanner acknowledged, not without pleasure, the nickname paternally bestowed on him long
ago by these men who had all been so much bigger than
he, who had chaffingly, unmaliciously treated him as their
mascot perhaps, because of his size, but had unswervingly
followed his direction. As a group they were still physically
impressive, carrying extra weight fairly well on their long
bones.

They gathered around to greet him. With the unfortunate
sobriety of the latecomer, he noted, accepting a drink, that
they were all, although not yet tipsy, a little relaxed, a
trifle suffused, with the larger-than-life voices and gestures
of men who had had a few. A table set buffet style in a
corner, and a coffee urn, had apparently not yet been
touched. Downing his first drink, he took another, and
plunged into the babble of expected questions, the "where
you been all these years?" — the "whaf're you doing now?"
— the "whereabouts you living?" One by one he remembered them all, even to the little personal tricks and ways
they had had in the locker-room. Bates, whose enormous
sweaty feet had been a loud joke with them all, was almost
completely bald now, as was Goetschius, the polite quiet

boy from upstate, who, politely as ever, bent his tonsure over Banks' pictures of his house, his family.

Reassuringly, they all looked pretty good, as he thought he did himself, but he wondered if they knew any better than he did what had impelled them to come. "Horse" Chernowski, who stood nearest him, had driven up from Pennsylvania, beckoned on, Spanner wondered, by what urge to reasseverate the past? In his ill-cut, too thick tweeds, his great shoulders swollen needlessly by shoulder pads, the hocklike wrist bones projecting from the cuffs — his nickname fitted him still. He had been their dumb baby, stronger than any of the others, but dull of reaction; once they had lost a race because of his slowness in going over the side when he had jammed his slide.

"Ah, my God, Davy," said Chernowski delightedly, "do you remember the cops picking us up for speeding after the big day — the night we drove back from Poughkeepsie?"

"Yes. Sure I remember," said Spanner, but he hadn't, until then. From across the room he saw Anderson, the stroke, nursing his drink at the mantel, staring at him ruefully, almost comprehendingly; encountering that blue gaze which had faced him steadily, in the inarticulate intimacy of three years of gruelling practice, faraway incident, and triumph, there was much that he did remember.

Handsome, intelligent son of a family which had contributed both money and achievement to the college for more than one generation, Anderson had more perfectly straddled the continuum of campus approval that stretched between "grind" and "hero" than anyone Spanner had known. Spanner remembered him, effortlessly debonair and assured, burnished hair spotlighted over the satin knee breeches of his costume as Archer in *The Beaux' Stratagem,* or stripped and white-lipped, holding Spanner's gaze with his own as the water seared past the shell. Although he had been as perilously near the prototype of campus hero as one could be without stuffiness or lampoonery, there had never been any of the glib sheen of the fair-haired boy about him, nothing in the just courtesy of his manner except the measurable flow of a certain *noblesse oblige.*

He crossed now to Spanner, and took, rather than shook, Spanner's hand.

"Davy!" he said. "Well, Davy!"

The crisp intonation had the same ease, the ruddy hair had merely faded to tan, the eyes stared down at him now straight as ever, but from between lids with the faint, flawed pink of the steady drinker, and Spanner saw now that there was in his posture the controlled waver, the scarcely perceptible imbalance of the man who is always quietly, competently drunk.

"You look fine, Davy," he said, smiling.

"You look fine too, Bob."

"Sure. Oh sure," he said, with a wry, self-derisive grimace. He indicated with his drink. "Look at us. Everyone looks fine. Householders all. Hard to believe we were the gents who took it full in the belly — depression, social consciousness." His accent was a little slurred now. "And wars and pestilence," he said more firmly. "Even if we were a little late for that." He downed his drink.

"You in the war, Bob?" said Spanner, somewhat lamely.

"Me? Not me," he said. "My kids were. Lost one — over

Germany." He walked over to the buffet, poured himself
a drink, and was back, swiftly. "Sounds antiquated already,
doesn't it? Over Germany. We're back to saying 'in Germany' now." He went on quickly, as if he had a speech in
mind that he would hold back if he thought it over.

"Remember the house I used to belong to? 'Bleak House,'
they used to call it, sometimes, remember? The one that got
into the news in the thirties because they hung a swastika
over the door. Or maybe somebody hung it on *them*." He
drank again. "Could have been either way," he said.

Spanner nodded. He had begun to be sick of the word
"remember"; it seemed as if everyone, including his self
of the night before, was intent on poking up through the
golden unsplit waters of his youth the sudden sharp fin of
some submerged reality, undefined, but about to become
clear.

"They were a nice bunch of fellows in our time," said
Spanner.

"You know . . . Davy . . ." Anderson said. His voice
trailed off. The fellow was apologetic; in his straight blue
look there was a hint of guilt, of shame, as if he too, the
previous night, had half dreamed and pondered, but unlike
Spanner had met the dark occupant of his dreamings face to
face.

"I wanted them to take you in," Anderson said. "A few of us
together could have pushed it through — but all the others
made such a God-damned stink about it, we gave in. I suppose you heard." He looked at Spanner, mistaking the latter's
unresponsiveness for accusation perhaps, and went on.

"If we hadn't all been so damned unseeing, so sure of ourselves in those days . . ." He broke off. "Ah well," he said, "that's water over the dam." And grasping Spanner's shoulders, he looked down at him in an unsteady bid for forgiveness, just before he released him with a brotherly slap on the back, and turned away, embarrassed. Standing there, it was as if Spanner felt the flat of it, not between his shoulder blades, but stinging on his suddenly hot cheek — that sharp slap of revelation.

The Woman
Who Was Everybody

At a quarter of eight, young Miss Abel was prodded out of sleep as usual by the harsh clanging of the bell in the church around the corner. It went on for as much as forty or fifty times, each clank plummeting instantly into silence, as if someone were beating iron against a stone. She did not get up at once, but lay there, seeing herself rise with the precision of a somnambulist, go from bathroom to kitchenette in the blind actions which would dissolve the sediment of sleep still in her eyes, in her bones. In her throat, a sick resistance to the day had already begun its familiar mounting, the pulse of a constant ache on which sleep had put only a delusory quietus. Lying there, she wondered which unwitting day of the past had been the one on which she must have exchanged the bright morning dower of childhood, that indolent assurance that the day was a nimbus of possibilities, for this heavy ache that collected in the throat like a catarrhal reminder that as yesterday was dusty, so would be today.

There had been nothing in her childhood, certainly, to warrant that early dowered expectancy, nothing in the girlhood spent in her mother's rooming house near that part of the Delaware River consecrated to the Marcus Hook refineries, where the great fungoid tanks bloomed oppressively over all, draining the frontal streets like theirs, which were neither country lanes nor town blocks, but only in-between passageways where the privet died hardily, without either pavement or neon to console one for its death. In that bland, unimpassioned climate the days had been blurred exhalations of the factories, the river and the people, dragging on into a darkness that was like the fainter, sooted, interchangeable breath of all of these. Perhaps the days had rung with expectancy for her, nevertheless, because from the first, for as long as she could remember, she had been so sure of getting out, away. As, of course, she had.

She swung sideways out of bed and clamped her feet on the floor, rose and trundled to the bathroom, the kitchenette. Boiled coffee was the quickest and most economical; watching the grounds spray and settle on the bubbling water, she took comfort from the small action. Everywhere in New York now toasters clicked, clocks rang, and people rising under the weight of the new day took heart from each little milestone of routine, like children, walking past a strange paling, who touch placatingly every third picket, hoping this will bring them through safe.

Fumbling without choice for one of the two dresses of the daily requisite black, she peered out the window into the alley beyond. The slick gray arms of the dwarfed tree, which grew, anonymous and mineral, from its humus of dust and concrete, were charitably fuzzed with light, and above them the water tanks and girders of the roofs beyond stood out against the fine yellow morning, clarified and glistening. Night could still down the city, absorbing it for all its rhinestone effrontery, but the mornings crept in like applicants for jobs, nuzzling humbly against the masked granite, saying hopefully, "Do you suppose . . . is there anything to be made of me?"

Behind her, except for the unmade bed, the room had the fierce, wooden neatness of the solitary, beginning house-holder. She turned from the window and made up the bed ₅swiftly so that the immobile room might greet her so, with all its rigid charm of permanence, at nightfall. Now there was nothing out of place except the letter from her mother, read and left crumpled on the table the night before.

None of the rooms in the house at Marcus Hook had ever really belonged to her mother, her sister Pauline or herself. The changing needs of the roomers came first — the work-men who had a wife coming or a wife leaving, the spinsters who made a religion of drafts and the devotional bath, the elderly male and female waifs who had to "retrench" farther and farther back into the cheapest recesses of the house, un-til the final retrenchment, to the home of a relative, could be delayed no longer.

The family, forever shifting, took what was left over. The best times would have been when the three of them slept in the big front sitting-room together, had not these also been the bad periods when the larger rooms went begging, and they and the most unimportant, delinquent roomer were almost on the same footing. But at all times, mornings the kitchen was never clear of "privilegers," evenings the parlor creaked and sighed with those for whom solitude was the worst of privileges. And late at night when, in no matter what bed or room one might be, there was still the padding in the corridors, the leakage of faucets, then the house rumored its livelihood most plainly of all, having no being other than in the sneaked murmurs, the soft crepitations of strangers.

She sipped the coffee, ate a roll, smoothing out her mother's letter. "Mrs. Tregarthen, she lived in New York once, says you are down in a terrible neighborhood and for the same money you could get into a business girls club. The Tregarthens still have the sitting-room thank God. I am so glad you are fixed in the Section Manager job, all that time you studied was not wasted after all. They say even the elevator girls have to be college now. You must be on your feet a lot too, be sure you have the proper shoes. Will you use the store discount and buy Pauline a white dress for graduation, size 14, something not fancy I can dye later. Let me know how much. I am so glad of the discount."

No use to explain again to her mother that she could only buy dark "employee" clothes for herself on the discount. She would send Pauline the dress and take care of the difference herself. All the four years of her scholarship her mother had worked to help her out, in mingled pride and worry over this queer chick who asked nothing better than to waste her real good looks over the books, after something, God knows what all, except that you could be sure it was something that couldn't be touched or twisted to use, and at best could only be taught. Her mother had been right. The year she was graduated Ph.D.'s were a dime a dozen, and the colleges had still less use for Miss Abel, A.B. She had learned that "getting out" meant, sooner or later, having to "get in" somewhere else. But her mother was pleased, now that she was fixed in her job. And glad of the discount.

Now that she was ready, she stared possessively at the safe shell of the room, all she had been able to salvage of her dream of solitary, inviolate pursuit. Each morning she had to resist the binding urge to stay, nestled in familiarity. She forced herself to put her hand on the knob of the outer door, meanwhile contrarily building up the temptation of the ideal day. Projecting herself into the reassuring feel of the chair, she saw herself settled there for hours, retreated into the subtle stream of a book, hugging emotions siphoned through another's words, immolating herself happily on the altar of a problem, an impasse, which might be dropped as one awakens from a dream, with the closing of the book. She wrenched the door open quickly and shut it behind her, giving it a shake to test the lock.

Once outside, she felt lighthearted, the decision for that day, at least, being over. Down here the neighborhood eased itself into living with the unconstraint of a slattern who has no plans. Across the street, in front of the Olive Tree Inn for Homeless Men, one of the flophouses run by the city, a few rumpled bums lounged like fallen dolls, staring vacantly with their frayed, inoffensive look. They were the safest people in the world to live among, she thought, for one could no more focus on their identities than they on the world around them; in their eyes there was never the shrewd look of the striving, but only the bleared gentleness of humiliation, and their dreams were not of women.

As she walked the long blocks westward to the BMT, the streets filled with people who had the crisp silhouette of destination, but as she neared them, going down the subway stairs, she could see the mouths still swollen with the unreserve of sleep, under the eyes the endearing childish puffs of the rudely awakened. Since she was travelling uptown against the morning rush, she got a seat almost at once and, settling into it, looked at the people opposite, who bobbed up and down with the blank withdrawal of the subwayite. Some mornings, translating them into their animal counterparts, she returned to the lidded stare immured in the bravely rouged, batrachian folds of some old harridan, traced the patient, naglike decline of a nose, watched the gibbon antics of the wizened messengers of the garment district as they pushed their eternally harrying, dwarfing packages. Once inside the store where she worked, exposed to them "on the floor," they all became the customer, the enemy, sauntering along freely in their enviably uncaged day, striking at her with the inimical, demanding shafts of their eyes, but here, until then, she could feel a wave of tenderness, of identification with them, which possessed her with a pity that included herself.

Thinking of the varied jobs toward which the people in the car were travelling, she remembered the prying regard of Miss Shotwell, the head of the store's "interviewing," and heard again the chill beads of words which had dropped from the deceptive, ductile bloom of her face.

"We can get any number of college graduates these days. We're only interested in those with a real vocation for merchandising." The protuberant eyes scrutinized with a glance which seemed to come from the whole eyeball.

"I worked in a store for a year before I went to college. And all my summer jobs were in department stores." She had sat there quietly, trying to shine with vocation, but thinking of those sweating miserable summers which had helped make possible the long winter hibernations in the libraries, she had wished herself back among the books, feeling the nausea of the displaced.

"H'mmm." The sedulously fluffed hair bent over the folder on the desk between them. "Your extracurricular leadership record was really very good." The head cocked to one side as if deliberating an article of purchase, then bent to the folder again in a gesture either habitual or posed, for the folder was closed. "Philosophy major, fine arts minor. That's not so good. We'd rather have it business administration, let's say, or mathematics."

"Something — more concrete?"

"Exactly," said Miss Shotwell, bringing her head back to center, her face obviously readied for the fulsome courtesies of rejection.

Behind the chic camouflage of her own smart appearance, that slick armor which she had learned to assume with the wiliness of the job-hunter, she had felt shaken with hatred for these people who had the power to let you in, who could annihilate, with a dainty, deprecatory finger, spheres of value which were not their own.

"It does not seem to have impaired my 'leadership,' as you

call it," she had said at last, anger forcing the gassy word on to her tongue.

The flickering interest had revived in the fish stare opposite. Miss Shotwell had smiled almost in approval. "Perhaps we can use you after all," she had said. "We like them to be aggressive."

Them. In the past year she had indeed become one of "them," learning the caitiff acquiescence, the shiny readiness which would cover the segration of self, acquiring that whole vocabulary of pretense forced upon those who must make themselves commercially valuable, or die.

She looked around now at the others herded together with her in the car. Perhaps her mistake had been to think that she was alone in this; perhaps each of her neighbors was sitting stiffened in the same intent misery before the deadening span of the day to come, each crouched protectively over the misfit hunch or sore of some disparity which had not fitted in. She looked again, but the set faces looked back at hers stonily, as if not all the prying tentacles of her pity could slip behind the mask which each had assumed for his journey through the ambuscade of the practical. Bending her head over the interlocked hands in her lap, she loosened them, cupped them softly over the unwanted extrusion of her compassion. *Everybody*, she said to herself in tentative kinship, each one of them, of *us*, locked up alone with the felony of his private difference.

The car rocked to her station and she pressed out with the others, up the stairs into a brief interlude of sunshine and into the swinging door of the employee's entrance, kept constantly ajar by the procession of batting hands.

Inside the olive green locker room she found the number of her own compartment and set her hat and coat away, smelling with a dull sense of recognition the basement's odor of wax and disinfectant, interfused with the vague patchouli of congregated women. One after the other, as they took off the bright spring hats and coats which had differentiated them up to now, they sank into conformity, leveled by the common denominator of their dark dresses as if by the command of some sullen alchemist.

Nodding diffidently to the few she knew by sight, she joined them on the escalator to the main floor, her spirits sinking as she rose. Upstairs in the glove department where she had been assistant section manager for the past two months, the salesgirls lounged negligently behind the counters, waiting for the opening bell to ring and the first trickle of customers.

"Good morning," she said.

"'Morning, Miss Abel." They were polite but reserved, with the resentment of old stagers who see a neophyte brought in to supervise.

"Miss Baxter in yet?" She asked only to make conversation, but was warned by their suddenly innocent gazes. Baxter must have come in drunk again.

"She's behind — in the cubbyhole," said one of the girls, and bent over, stifling a snicker.

Behind the counter there was a door which led into the cavity under the escalator, a space big enough for two people if one sat in the single chair and the other stood with head bent under the declivity of the ceiling. The girls seldom used it, ducking in for an aspirin, or when a garter had broken and there was not time to go off the floor. Once or twice, when the hysteria of milling people around her had overwhelmed her with a feeling of nakedness, of exposure to too much and too many, she had crept in there herself for a moment of poise. She opened the door and went in, closing it behind her.

Miss Baxter sat erect in the single chair, her angular shoulders squared tensely in one of the severely cut suits she wore daily. Miss Abel had never known her to wear a dress. Her cropped black hair was sleek from the brush, and her starched white shirt lay flat and crisp under one of the ties she affected, the cuffs projecting slightly from the jacket sleeves to show the only touch of vanity she allowed herself, onyx intaglio cuff links which clipped together like a man's. With her firm, pallid profile and small, almost lipless mouth, she had the anomalous attractiveness of a well-groomed boy who is knowing and bitter beyond his years. Reputed to be the best section manager on the floor, she had been recruited temporarily from the enormous book department to cover the glove section during the spring rush. Once or twice Miss Abel, longing for congeniality, had tried to get her to talk about books, of which she was supposed to have considerable knowledge, but had been not so much rebuffed as forestalled by the controlled distance of manner, the look of careful mistrust in the deep-set eyes.

Miss Baxter grasped her own chin in one hand and gravely swung her head to one side, then back. "I daren't move it by itself," she said in her husky whisky voice. Staring straight ahead, she uncurled the other hand in her lap to show a package of Life Savers. "Have one?" she said without moving further, and laughed.

"Can I get you anything?" Miss Abel put out a hand, but somehow she did not dare touch her.

In answer Miss Baxter, still sitting erect, closed her eyes. "What a night!" she said. "Lois' job is folding, so we went on the town." The words came oddly from the closed face, with a kind of bravado perhaps made possible by it. "Know Lois Gow, up in the doctor's office?"

"Oh. Yes, of course." She remembered the girl mainly because of the pliant, hesitant manner which did not go with the nurse's uniform, and the suffused pink of her face, which always looked as if she were about to sneeze or break into tears.

"Think I can go on the floor, Abel?" Miss Baxter had opened her eyes, and was looking straight at her with her thin, slight smile. Except for the closed eyes, she had seemed up to now almost as she had on those other mornings when, rigidly controlled, exuding a powerful perfume of cinnamon, she had managed quite competently, handling both staff and customers with a dispatch which was, if anything, chillier than normal. But now, looking into the opened eyes, Miss Abel saw that the liquor had not glazed them but rather had melted from them some last cornea of reserve, so that, nude and pained, they focused beyond her, askance at some unalterable incubus.

"Look," said Miss Abel, "you've signed in, haven't you? Why don't you go to the rest room? I can cover up for you here."

Miss Baxter shook herself slightly. With that shake, policy shuttered her face and she was again the equilibrist, the authority.

"Quite a gal, aren't you?" she said. "Able Abel." She laughed. Then she put her head in her hands.

Miss Abel went out and closed the door behind her. Hurrying to the high desk behind which she would stand all day, she began needlessly to set its sparse equipment in order. She couldn't have gone on the floor, she said to herself. Not with those eyes.

The rest of the morning she worked steadily to reduce the constantly forming queue of women in front of her. Just before noon, a cool voice said, "I'll take over now. Thanks." Miss Baxter stood beside her, resurrected and remote.

Miss Abel got her purse from the desk, signed out and left the floor. Outside the locker-room windows the day had turned greenish and it had begun to drizzle. She had no heart for battling one of the crowded restaurants outside and turned into the employees' cafeteria, where she ate her way through the flaccid "special plate," flavored for the general and made more tepid by the humid smell from the steam tables. Gratefully she remembered that it was Saturday and, half-reluctantly, she visualized her usual date with Max.

As on many other Saturday nights, she would prepare dinner for him, and they would sit over it in a coy, uncomfortable imitation of the domesticity they could not afford to make actual. If, during the past week, he had been called for part-time work in one of the biological-testing laboratories which allowed him, as a former fellow in chemistry, to make tests of blood and sputum, they would go to one of the movies on Fourteenth Street. Otherwise, while he talked ardently of his ambitions, his hopes, warming his self-confidence with her attention, she would watch the light on the humbled nape of his neck, the abnormal cleanliness of his hands, seeing in them something already intimidated, subdued. Either way, she thought, it would end in the half-fearful, fending love-making of the uninitiate, in that tentative groping, not toward affirmation but only toward escape, in which each caressed and comforted the affrighted, sad replica of himself.

She rose with a counterfeit briskness and went back upstairs. Signing in again, "Abel — 12:45," she slipped into her station beside Miss Baxter.

At five o'clock when the two of them, working steadily together, had disposed of the last of the queue, the crowd in the store had thinned. It was raining hard outside now, and most of the customers, wandering along desultory and vacant-faced, were of the brand the clerks called "just looking." Miss Abel and Miss Baxter stood together behind the high pulpit of the desk, careful not to mar with more than fragmentary conversation their air of alert, executive readiness.

Along the aisle a small, nondescript woman teetered aimlessly toward them. She was no different from the scores of women who had today — and would tomorrow — filtered colorlessly through the store from the cardboard suburbs or the moderately respectable crannies of the city. A coat of some nameless but adequate fur flapped back from a dress which was indistinctly neither fussy nor smart. On her precise, mat hair a small flyaway hat with a veil halfway between coquetry and conservatism perched sharply to one side — denotation that its wearer might have lost touch with her sense of the ridiculous but not with her instinct for what was correct for her station in life. Beloved of some man, she would amble through the stores, coming home with a darling blouse or another pair of stubby, frilled shoes, or perhaps only with a sense of virtue at having viewed and resisted all the temptations of the *bon marché* except the paper bag of caramels from which she was now munching.

She stopped in front of them, just to one side, and stared frankly, curiously at Miss Baxter. Then, with her face screwed up in kittenish perplexity, she backed up, sidestepped, craned over to get a glimpse of Miss Baxter's legs.

"Is there something I can do for you?" There was an edge of insolence in Miss Baxter's tone which made Miss Abel catch her breath with apprehension. Sidling a glance from under the dropped lids of embarrassment, she saw what she had never before seen in Miss Baxter's face — the creeping red of color.

"Well, uh, no." The woman tittered ingratiatingly. "I mean — I just couldn't tell whether — I mean I just wanted to see . . . whether you had *trousers* on," she finished, the words coming out on a cozy gust of confidence. She smiled, and tittered again.

"Want to step around and take a really good look?" Miss Baxter's face was white again.

"Why, you — why, this is *outrageous!*" Rage did not dignify the woman's inadequate features. "Why, I could *report* you!"

"Get out." Miss Baxter's immobility was more offensive than her words.

"I'll report you for this!" Looking around for adherents, the woman met the bright, hushed stare of the clerks. Drawing her coat around her, she stalked off, her face working and mottled, the paper bag crackling convulsively in her hand.

She will, too, thought Miss Abel. She kept her glance carefully apart from Miss Baxter. The clerks, heads bent ostentatiously over their books, returned to their tallying of the day's receipts.

With a thin, releasing sound, the five-thirty bell rang through the store. If I tell Baxter to get out quickly, she won't, thought Miss Abel. She said nothing. After a face-saving moment, Miss Baxter opened the desk drawer slowly and took out her purse.

"My turn to close up," said Miss Abel. "Good night."

" 'Night," said Miss Baxter. She hesitated for a moment as if there were something she wanted to say, then gave a half-smile, as if the concession shamed her, and left.

Methodically Miss Abel set the desk to rights for Monday morning. Baxter had left without signing out. As she signed the chart for both of them with a grim feeling of conspiracy, she saw Mr. Eardley, the floor superintendent, a sandy-haired, middle-aged man with tiredly pleasant manners, being pulled toward her down the aisle by the gesticulating woman. They stopped in front of her.

"She isn't here," said the woman. "This girl will tell you, though. The idea!"

"Yes, Madam." Mr. Eardley looked at Miss Abel, his brows raised over his glasses in weary inquiry.

Miss Abel looked at the woman. She was still babbling angrily to Mr. Eardley and her silly hat, held on by elastic, was cocked awry on her head, far beyond the angle of fashion. Even the exertions of her annoyance had not been able to endow her with individuality, but under stress the details of her person, so dependent on the commonplace, appeared disorderly, even daft.

Miss Abel looked past her at Mr. Eardley. Imperceptibly she shook her head and, raising her hand to her temple, she moved her index finger discreetly in the small circle, the immemorial gesture of derision.

As if he had caught a ball deftly thrown, Mr. Eardley nodded imperceptibly back. Turning quickly toward the woman, he burbled the smooth reassurances of his trade. He took note of her name and address in a voice which was soothing and deferential, and on a wave of practiced apologies he urged the woman inexorably toward the door.

Miss Abel walked down to the basement once more on one of the escalators which had stopped for the day, got her hat and coat and a spare umbrella from her locker and left the store. Under the jaundiced cast of the rain the faces of the people on the street looked froglike and repellent. In the subway she sat numbly in a catalepsy of fatigue, her feet squirming in her soggy, drenched shoes. She walked the long blocks from the station at a blind pace, the umbrella slanted viciously in front of her, her mind fixed on the chair at home.

At last she was there, and the dead, still air of the apartment welcomed her, inspiring a relief close to tears. Dropping off her damp clothes and soaked shoes, she put on a wrapper and mules and set a pot of water to boil. Usually when she came home she had cup after cup of dark coffee, but now the thought of its flavor, hearty and congenial, sickened her. Tea, meliorative and astringent, recalled those childhood convalescences when it had been the first sign of recovery, and half-medicine, half-food, it had settled the stomach and warmed the hands. She set a pot of tea to steep, brought the tray around in front of the chair and sat down. After a moment she kicked off the slippers with a dual thud which was like a signal to thought.

Looking back on the day, she curled her lip at the mawkish sentiments of that morning in the train, at the nascent fellowship which had seemed so plausible. The day seemed now like a labyrinth through which she had followed an infallible, an educative thread — to a monster's door.

Everybody, she thought, shivering. The woman in the store was "everybody." Multiplied endlessly, she and her counterparts, varied slightly by the secondary markings of sex, education, money, flowed in and out of the stores, in and out of all the proper stations in life, not touched by the miseries of difference but indomitably chewing the caramel cud of their own self-satisfaction. Escape into the long dream of books, behind the ramparts of your special talent or into some warm coterie of your own ilk, and they could still find you out with a judgment in proportion to the degree of your difference. The Misses Baxter they would pillory at once, with the nerveless teamwork of the dull; the Misses Abel might escape their gray encroaching smutch of averageness for a while, behind some *maquillage* of compromise, only to find one day perhaps that the *maquillage* had become the spirit — that they had conquered after all.

They were even there, latent, in the rumpled letter, simple with love, still lying on her table. In the end they could push everything before them with the nod of their terrible consanguinity.

She moved deeper in the chair. Soon the boy, Max, would come, and in the desperate wrenches, the muffled clingings of love-making they would try again to build up some dark mutual core of inalienable wholeness. For there was no closeness, she thought, no camaraderie so intense, so tempting as that of the rejected for the rejected. But in the end those others would still be there to be faced; in the end they were to be faced alone. Meanwhile she sat on, shivering a little, over the steaming tea, and making a circle of her body around the hardening nugget of herself, she clasped her chill, blanched feet in her slowly warming hands.

Heartburn

THE light, gritty wind of a spring morning blew in on the doctor's shining, cleared desk, and on the tall buttonhook of a man who leaned agitatedly toward him.

"I have some kind of small animal lodged in my chest," said the man. He coughed, a slight, hollow apologia to his ailment, and sank back in his chair.

"Animal?" said the doctor, after a pause which had the unfortunate quality of comment. His voice, however, was practiced, deft, colored only with the careful suspension of judgment.

"Probably a form of newt or toad," answered the man, speaking with clipped distaste, as if he would disassociate himself from the idea as far as possible. His face quirked with sad foreknowledge. "Of course, you don't believe me."

The doctor looked at him noncommittally. Paraphrased, an old refrain of the poker table leapt erratically in his mind. "Nits" — no — "newts and gnats and one-eyed jacks," he thought. But already the anecdote was shaping itself, trim and perfect, for display at the clinic luncheon table. "Go on," he said.

"Why won't any of you come right out and say what you think!" the man said angrily. Then he flushed, not hectically, the doctor noted, but with the well-bred embarrassment of the normally reserved. "Sorry. I didn't mean to be rude."

"You've already had an examination?" The doctor was a neurologist, and most of his patients were referrals.

"My family doctor. I live up in Boston."

"Did you tell him — er . . . ?" The doctor sought gingerly for a phrase.

One corner of the man's mouth lifted, as if he had watched others in the same dilemma. "I went through the routine first. Fluoroscope, metabolism, cardiograph. Even gastroscopy." He spoke, the doctor noted, with the regrettable glibness of the patient who has shopped around.

"And — the findings?" said the doctor, already sure of the answer.

The man leaned forward, holding the doctor's glance with his own. A faint smile riffled his mouth. "Positive."

"Positive!"

"Well," said the man, "machines have to be interpreted after all, don't they?" He attempted a shrug, but the quick eye of the doctor saw that the movement masked a slight contortion within his tweed suit, as if the man writhed away from himself but concealed it quickly, as one masks a hiccup with a cough. "A curious flutter in the cardiograph, a strange variation in the metabolism, an alien shadow under the fluoroscope." He coughed again and put a genteel hand over his mouth, but this time the doctor saw it clearly — the slight, cringing motion.

"You see," added the man, his eyes helpless and apologetic above the polite covering hand. "It's alive. It *travels*."

"Yes. Yes, of course," said the doctor, soothingly now. In his mind hung the word, ovoid and perfect as a drop of water about to fall. Obsession. A beautiful case. He thought again of the luncheon table.

"What did your doctor recommend?" he said.

"A place with more resources, like the Mayo Clinic. It was then that I told him I knew what it was, as I've told you. And how I acquired it." The visitor paused. "Then, of course, he was forced to pretend he believed me."

"Forced?" said the doctor.

"Well," said the visitor, "actually, I think he did believe me. People tend to believe anything these days. All this mass media information gives them the habit. It takes a strong individual to disbelieve evidence."

The doctor was confused and annoyed. Well, "What then?" he said peremptorily, ready to rise from his desk in dismissal.

Again came the fleeting bodily grimace and the quick cough. "He — er . . . he gave me a prescription."

The doctor raised his eyebrows, in a gesture he was swift to retract as unprofessional.

"For heartburn, I think it was," added his visitor demurely.

Tipping back in his chair, the doctor tapped a pencil on the edge of the desk. "Did he suggest you seek help — on another level?"

"Many have suggested it," said the man.

"But I'm not a psychiatrist!" said the doctor irritably.

"Oh, I know that. You see, I came to you because I had the luck to hear one of your lectures at the Academy. The one on 'Overemphasis on the Non-somatic Causes of Nervous Disorder.' It takes a strong man to go against the tide like that. A disbeliever. And that's what I sorely need." The visitor shuddered, this time letting the *frisson* pass uncontrolled. "You see," he added, thrusting his clasped hands forward on the desk, and looking ruefully at the doctor, as if he would cushion him against his next remark, "you see — I am a psychiatrist."

The doctor sat still in his chair.

"Ah, I can't help knowing what you are thinking," said the man. "I would think the same. A streamlined version of the Napoleonic delusion." He reached into his breast pocket, drew out a wallet, and fanned papers from it on the desk.

"Never mind. I believe you!" said the doctor hastily.

"Already?" said the man sadly.

Reddening, the doctor hastily looked over the collection of letters, cards of membership in professional societies, licenses, and so on — very much the same sort of thing he himself would have had to amass, had he been under the same necessity of proving his identity. Sanity, of course, was another matter. The documents were all issued to Dr. Curtis Retz at a Boston address. Stolen, possibly, but something in the man's manner, in fact everything in it except his unfortunate hallucination, made the doctor think otherwise. Poor guy, he thought. Occupational fatigue, perhaps. But what a form! The Boston variant, possibly. "Suppose you start from the beginning," he said benevolently.

"If you can spare the time . . ."

"I have no more appointments until lunch." And what a lunch that'll be, the doctor thought, already cherishing the pop-eyed scene — Travis the clinic's director (that plethoric Nestor), and young Gruenberg (all of whose cases were unique), his hairy nostrils dilated for once in a *mise-en-scène* which he did not dominate.

Holding his hands pressed formally against his chest, almost in the attitude of one of the minor placatory figures in a *Pietà*, the visitor went on. "I have the usual private practice," he said, "and clinic affiliations. As a favor to an old friend of mine, headmaster of a boys' school nearby, I've acted as guidance consultant there for some years. The school caters to boys of above average intelligence and is run along progressive lines. Nothing's ever cropped up except run-of-the-mill adolescent problems, colored a little, perhaps, by the type of parents who tend to send their children to a school like that — people who are — well — one might say, almost tediously aware of their commitments as parents."

The doctor grunted. He was that kind of parent himself.

"Shortly after the second term began, the head asked me to come down. He was worried over a sharp drop of morale which seemed to extend over the whole school — general inattention in classes, excited note-passing, nightly disturbances in the dorms — all pointing, he had thought at first, to the existence of some fancier than usual form of hazing, or to one of those secret societies, sometimes laughable, sometimes with overtones of the corrupt, with which all schools are familiar. Except for one thing. One after the other, a long list of boys had been sent to the infirmary by the various teachers who presided in the dining room. Each of the boys had shown a marked debility, and what the resident doctor called 'All the stigmata of pure fright. Complete un-

willingness to confide.' Each of the boys pleaded stubbornly
for his own release, and a few broke out of their own accord.
The interesting thing was that each child did recover shortly
after his own release, and it was only after this that another
boy was seen to fall ill. No two were afflicted at the same
time."

"Check the food?" said the doctor.

"All done before I got there. According to my friend, all
the trouble seemed to have started with the advent of one
boy, John Hallowell, a kid of about fifteen, who had come
to the school late in the term with a history of having run
away from four other schools. Records at these classed him
as very bright, but made oblique references to 'personality
difficulties' which were not defined. My friend's school, ordinarily pretty independent, had taken the boy at the in-
sistence of old Simon Hallowell, the boy's uncle, who is a
trustee. His brother, the boy's father, is well known for
his marital exploits which have nourished the tabloids for
years. The mother lives mostly in France and South America.
One of these perennial dryads, apparently, with a youthful-
ness maintained by money and a yearly immersion in the
fountains of American plastic surgery. Only time she sees
the boy . . . Well, you can imagine. What the feature articles call a Broken Home."

The doctor shifted in his chair and lit a cigarette.

"I won't keep you much longer," said the visitor. "I saw
the boy." A violent fit of coughing interrupted him. This
time his curious writhing motion went frankly unconcealed.
He got up from his chair and stood at the window, gripping
the sill and breathing heavily until he had regained control,

and went on, one hand pulling unconsciously at his collar. "Or, at least, I think I saw him. On my way to visit him in his room I bumped into a tall red-headed boy in a football sweater, hurrying down the hall with a windbreaker and a poncho slung over his shoulder. I asked for Hallowell's room; he jerked a thumb over his shoulder at the door just behind him, and continued past me. It never occurred to me . . . I was expecting some adenoidal gangler with acne . . . or one of these sinister little angel faces, full of neurotic sensibility.

"The room was empty. Except for its finicky neatness, and a rather large amount of livestock, there was nothing unusual about it. The school, according to the current trend, is run like a farm, with the boys doing the chores, and pets are encouraged. There was a tank with a couple of turtles near the window, beside it another, full of newts, and in one corner a large cage of well-tended, brisk white mice. Glass cases, with carefully mounted series of lepidoptera and hymenoptera, showing the metamorphic stages, hung on the walls, and on a drawing board there was a daintily executed study of Branchippus, the 'fairy shrimp.'

"While I paced the room, trying to look as if I wasn't prying, a greenish little wretch, holding himself together as if he had an imaginary shawl draped around him, slunk into the half-dark room and squeaked 'Hallowell?' When he saw me he started to duck, but I detained him and found that he had had an appointment with Hallowell too. When it was clear, from his description, that Hallowell must have been the redhead I'd seen leaving, the poor urchin burst into tears.

" 'I'll never get rid of it now!' he wailed. From then on it wasn't hard to get the whole maudlin story. It seems that shortly after Hallowell's arrival at school he acquired a reputation for unusual proficiency with animals and for out-of-the way lore which would impress the ingenuous. He circulated the rumor that he could swallow small animals and regurgitate them at will. No one actually saw him swallow anything, but it seems that in some mumbo-jumbo with another boy who had shown cynicism about the whole thing, it was claimed that Hallowell had, well, divested himself of something, and passed it on to the other boy, with the statement that the latter would only be able to get rid of his cargo when he in turn found a boy who would disbelieve *him.*"

The visitor paused, calmer now, and leaving the window sat down again in the chair opposite the doctor, regarding him with such fixity that the doctor shifted uneasily, with the apprehension of one who is about to be asked for a loan.

"My mind turned to the elementary sort of thing we've all done at times. You know, circle of kids in the dark, piece of cooked cauliflower passed from hand to hand with the statement that the stuff is the fresh brains of some neophyte who hadn't taken his initiation seriously. My young informer, Moulton his name was, swore however that this hysteria (for of course, that's what I thought it) was passed on singly, from boy to boy, without any such séances. He'd been home to visit his family, who are missionaries on leave, and had been infected by his roommate on his return to school, unaware that by this time the whole school had protectively turned believers, en masse. His own terror came, not only from his conviction that he was possessed, but from his inability to find anybody who would take his dare. And so he'd finally come to Hallowell. . . .

"By this time the room was getting really dark and I snapped on the light to get a better look at Moulton. Except for an occasional shudder, like a bodily tic, which I took to be the aftereffects of hard crying, he looked like a healthy enough boy who'd been scared out of his wits. I remember that a neat little monograph was already forming itself in my mind, a group study on mass psychosis, perhaps, with effective anthropological references to certain savage tribes whose dances include a rite known as 'eating evil.'

"The kid was looking at me. 'Do you believe me?' he said suddenly. 'Sir?' he added, with a naive cunning which tickled me.

" 'Of course,' I said, patting his shoulder absently. 'In a way.'

"His shoulder slumped under my hand. I felt its tremor, direct misery palpitating between my fingers.

" 'I thought . . . maybe for a man . . . it wouldn't be . . .' His voice trailed off.

" 'Be the same? . . . I don't know,' I said slowly, for of course, I was answering, not his actual question, but the overtone of some cockcrow of meaning that evaded me.

"He raised his head and petitioned me silently with his eyes. Was it guile, or simplicity, in his look, and was it for conviction, or the lack of it, that he arraigned me? I don't know. I've gone back over what I did then, again and again, using all my own knowledge of the mechanics of decision, and I know that it wasn't just sympathy, or a pragmatic reversal of therapy, but something intimately important for me, that made me shout with all my strength — 'Of course I don't believe you!'

"Moulton, his face contorted, fell forward on me so suddenly that I stumbled backwards, sending the tank of newts crashing to the floor. Supporting him with my arms, I hung on to him while he heaved, face downwards. At the same time I felt a tickling, sliding sensation in my own ear, and an inordinate desire to follow it with my finger, but both my hands were busy. It wasn't a minute 'til I'd gotten him onto the couch, where he drooped, a little white about the mouth, but with that chastened, purified look of the physically relieved, although he hadn't actually upchucked.

"Still watching him, I stooped to clear up the debris, but he bounded from the couch with amazing resilience.

" 'I'll do it,' he said.

" 'Feel better?'

"He nodded, clearly abashed, and we gathered up the remains of the tank in a sort of mutual embarrassment. I can't remember that either of us said a word, and neither of us made more than a halfhearted attempt to search for the scattered pests which had apparently sought crannies in the room. At the door we parted, muttering as formal a goodnight as was possible between a grown man and a small boy. It wasn't until I reached my own room and sat down that I realized, not only my own extraordinary behavior, but that Moulton, standing, as I suddenly recalled, for the first time quite straight, had sent after me a look of pity and speculation.

"Out of habit, I reached into my breast pocket for my

pencil, in order to take notes as fresh as possible. And then I felt it . . . a skittering, sidling motion, almost beneath my hand. I opened my jacket and shook myself, thinking that I'd picked up something in the other room . . . but nothing. I sat quite still, gripping the pencil, and after an interval it came again — an inchoate creeping, a twitter of move-ment almost *lackadaisical,* as of something inching itself lazily along — but this time on my other side. In a frenzy, I peeled off my clothes, inspected myself wildly, and enumer-ating to myself a reassuring abracadabra of explanation — skipped heartbeat, intercostal pressure of gas — I sat there naked, waiting. And after a moment, it came again, that wandering, aquatic motion, as if something had flipped itself over just enough to make me aware, and then set-tled itself, this time under the sternum, with a nudge like that of some inconceivable foetus. I jumped up and shook myself again, and as I did so I caught a glimpse of my-self in the mirror in the closet door. My face, my own face, was ajar with fright, and I was standing there, hooked over, as if I were wearing an imaginary shawl."

In the silence after his visitor's voice stopped, the doctor sat there in the painful embarrassment of the listener who has played confessor, and whose expected comment is a responsibility he wishes he had evaded. The breeze from the open window fluttered the papers on the desk. Glancing out at the clean, regular façade of the hospital wing opposite, at whose evenly shaded windows the white shapes of or-derlies and nurses flickered in consoling routine, the doctor wished petulantly that he had fended off the man and all his papers in the beginning. What right had the man to arraign *him?* Surprised at his own inner vehemence, he pulled himself together. "How long ago?" he said at last.

"Four months."

"And since?"

"It's never stopped." The visitor now seemed brimming with a tentative excitement, like a colleague discussing a mutually puzzling case. "Everything's been tried. Sedatives do obtain some sleep, but that's all. Purgatives. Even emetics." He laughed slightly, almost with pride. "Nothing like that works," he continued, shaking his head with the doting fondness of a patient for some symptom which has confounded the best of them. "It's too cagey for that."

With his use of the word "it," the doctor was propelled back into that shapely sense of reality which had gone admittedly askew during the man's recital. To admit the category of "it," to dip even a slightly co-operative finger in another's fantasy, was to risk one's own equilibrium. Better not to become involved in argument with the possessed, lest one's own apertures of belief be found to have been left ajar.

"I am afraid," the doctor said blandly, "that your case is outside my field."

"As a doctor?" said his visitor. "Or as a man?"

"Let's not discuss me, if you please."

The visitor leaned intently across the desk. "Then you admit that to a certain extent, we *have* been — ?"

"I admit nothing!" said the doctor, stiffening.

"Well," said the man disparagingly, "of course, that too is a kind of stand. The commonest, I've found." He sighed, pressing one hand against his collarbone. "I suppose you have a prescription too, or a recommendation. Most of them do."

The doctor did not enjoy being judged. "Why don't you hunt up young Hallowell?" he said, with malice.

"Disappeared. Don't you think I tried?" said his vis-à-vis ruefully. Something furtive, hope, perhaps, spread its guileful corruption over his face. "That means you do give a certain credence — "

"Nothing of the sort!"

"Well then," said his interrogator, turning his palms upward.

The doctor leaned forward, measuring his words with exasperation. "Do you mean you *want* me to tell you you're crazy!"

"In my spot," answered his visitor meekly, "which would you prefer?"

Badgered to the point of commitment, the doctor stared back at his inconvenient Diogenes. Swollen with irritation, he was only half conscious of an uneasy, vestigial twitching of his ear muscles, which contracted now as they sometimes did when he listened to atonal music.

"O.K., O.K. . . !" he shouted suddenly, slapping his hand down on the desk and thrusting his chin forward. "Have it your way then! I don't believe you!"

Rigid, the man looked back at him cataleptically, seeming, for a moment, all eye. Then, his mouth stretching in that medieval grimace, risorial and equivocal, whose mask appears sometimes on one side of the stage, sometimes on the other, he fell forward on the desk, with a long, mewing sigh.

Before the doctor could reach him, he had raised himself on his arms and their foreheads touched. They recoiled, staring downward. Between them on the desk, as if one of its mahogany shadows had become animate, something seemed to move — small, seal-colored, and ambiguous. For a moment it filmed back and forth, arching in a crude, primordial inquiry; then, homing straight for the doctor, whose jaw hung down in a rictus of shock, it disappeared from view.

Sputtering, the doctor beat the air and his own person wildly with his hands, and staggered upward from his chair. The breeze blew hypnotically, and the stranger gazed back at him with such perverse calm that already he felt an assailing doubt of the lightning, untoward event. He fumbled back over his sensations of the minute before, but already piecemeal and chimerical, they eluded him now, as they might forever.

"It's unbelievable," he said weakly.

His visitor put up a warding hand, shaking it fastidiously. *"Au contraire!"* he replied daintily, as though by the use of another language he would remove himself still further from commitment. Reaching forward, he gathered up his papers into a sheaf, and stood up, stretching himself straight with an all-over bodily yawn of physical ease that was like an affront. He looked down at the doctor, one hand fingering his wallet. "No," he said reflectively, "guess not." He tucked the papers away. "Shall we leave it on the basis of — er — professional courtesy?" he inquired delicately.

Choking on the sludge of his rage, the doctor looked back at him, inarticulate.

Moving toward the door, the visitor paused. "After all," he said, "with your connections . . . try to think of it as a temporary inconvenience." Regretfully, happily, he closed the door behind him.

The doctor sat at his desk, humped forward. His hands crept to his chest and crossed. He swallowed, experimentally. He hoped it was rage. He sat there, waiting. He was thinking of the luncheon table.

A Wreath for Miss Totten

CHILDREN growing up in the country take their images of integrity from the land. The land, with its changes, is always about them, a pervasive truth, and their midget foregrounds are crisscrossed with minute dramas which are the animalcules of a larger vision. But children who grow in a city where there is nothing greater than the people brimming up out of subways, riveting in the streets — these children must take their archetypes where and if they find them.

In P.S. 146, between periods, when the upper grades were shunted through the halls in that important procedure known as "departmental," although most of the teachers stood about chatting relievedly in couples, Miss Totten always stood at the door of her "home room," watching us straightforwardly, alone. As, straggling and muffled, we lined past the other teachers, we often caught snatches of upstairs gossip which we later perverted and enlarged; passing before Miss Totten we deflected only that austere look, bent solely on us.

Perhaps, with the teachers, as with us, she was neither admired nor loathed but simply ignored. Certainly none of us ever fawned on her as we did on the harshly blond and blue-eyed Miss Steele, who never wooed us with a smile but slanged us delightfully in the gym, giving out the exercises in a voice like scuffed gravel. Neither did she obsess us in the way of the Misses Comstock, two liverish, stunted women who could have had nothing so vivid about them as our hatred for them, and though all of us had a raffish hunger for metaphor, we never dubbed Miss Totten with a nickname.

Miss Totten's figure, as she sat tall at her desk or strode angularly in front of us rolling down the long maps over the blackboard, had that instantaneous clarity, one metallic step removed from the real, of the daguerreotype. Her clothes partook of this period too — long, saturnine waists and skirts of a stuff identical with that in a good family umbrella. There was one like it in the umbrella-stand at home — a high black one with a seamed ivory head. The waists enclosed a vestee of dim, but steadfast lace; the skirts grazed narrow boots of that etiolated black leather, venerable with creases, which I knew to be a sign both of respectability and foot trouble. But except for the vestee, all of Miss Totten, too, folded neatly to the dark point of her shoes, and separated from these by her truly extraordinary length, her face presided above, a lined, ocher ellipse. Sometimes, as I watched it on drowsy afternoons, her face floated away altogether and came to rest on the stand at home. Perhaps it was because of this guilty image that I was the only one who noticed Miss Totten's strange preoccupation with "Mooley" Davis.

Most of us in Miss Totten's room had been together as a group since first grade, but we had not seen Mooley since down in second grade, under the elder and more frightening of the two Comstocks. I had forgotten Mooley completely, but when she reappeared I remembered clearly the incident which had given her her name.

That morning, very early in the new term, back in Miss Comstock's, we had lined up on two sides of the classroom for a spelling bee. These were usually a relief to good and bad spellers alike, since it was the only part of our work which resembled a game, and even when one had to miss and sit down, there was a kind of dreamy catharsis in watching the tenseness of those still standing. Miss Comstock always rose for these occasions and came forward between the two lines, standing there in an oppressive close-up in which we could watch the terrifying action of the cords in her spindling gray neck and her slight smile as a boy or a girl was spelled down. As the number of those standing was reduced, the smile grew, exposing the oversize slabs of her teeth, through which the words issued in a voice increasingly unctuous and soft.

On this day the forty of us still shone with the first fall neatness of new clothes, still basked in that delightful anonymity in which neither our names nor our capacities were already part of the dreary foreknowledge of the teacher. The smart and quick had yet to assert themselves with their flying, staccato hands; the uneasy dull, not yet forced into recitations which would make their status clear, still preserved in the small, sinking corners of their hearts a lorn, factitious hope. Both teams were still intact when the word

"mule" fell to the lot of a thin colored girl across the room
from me, in clothes perky only with starch, her rusty fuzz
of hair drawn back in braids so tightly sectioned that her
eyes seemed permanently widened.

"Mule," said Miss Comstock, giving out the word. The
ranks were still full. She had not yet begun to smile.

The girl looked back at Miss Comstock, soundlessly. All
her face seemed drawn backward from the silent, working
mouth, as if a strong, pulling hand had taken hold of the
braids.

My turn, I calculated, was next. The procedure was to say
the word, spell it out, and say it again. I repeated it in my
mind: "Mule. M-u-l-e. Mule."

Miss Comstock waited quite a long time. Then she looked
around the class, as if asking them to mark well and early
this first malfeasance, and her handling of it.

"What's your name?" she said.

"Ull — ee." The word came out in a glottal, molasses voice,
hardly articulate, the *l*'s scarcely pronounced.

"Lilly?"

The girl nodded.

"Lilly what?"

"Duh-avis."

"Oh. Lilly Davis. Mmmm. Well, spell 'mule,' Lilly." Miss
Comstock trilled out the name beautifully.

The tense brown bladder of the girl's face swelled desperately, then broke at the mouth. "Mool," she said, and
stopped. "Mmm — oo — "

The room tittered. Miss Comstock stepped closer.

"Mule!"

The girl struggled again. "Mool."

This time we were too near Miss Comstock to dare laughter.

Miss Comstock turned to our side. "Who's next?"

I half raised my hand.

"Go on." She wheeled around on Lilly, who was sinking into her seat. "No. Don't sit down."

I lowered my eyelids, hiding Lilly from my sight. "Mule," I said. "M-u-l-e. Mule."

The game continued, words crossing the room uneventfully. Some children survived. Others settled, abashed, into their seats, craning around to watch us. Again the turn came around to Lilly.

Miss Comstock cleared her throat. She had begun to smile. "Spell it now, Lilly," she said. "Mule."

The long-chinned brown face swung from side to side in an odd writhing movement. Lilly's eyeballs rolled. Then the thick sound from her mouth was lost in the hooting, uncontrollable laughter of the whole class. For there was no doubt about it: the long, coffee-colored face, the whitish glint of the eyeballs, the bucking motion of the head suggested it to us all — a small brown quadruped, horse or mule, crazily stubborn, or at bay.

"Quiet!" said Miss Comstock. And we hushed, although she had not spoken loudly. For the word had smirked out from a wide, flat smile and on the stringy neck beneath there was a creeping, pleasurable flush which made it pink as a young girl's.

That was how Mooley Davis got her name, although we had a chance to use it only for a few weeks, in a taunting singsong when she hung up her coat in the morning, or as she flicked past the little dust-bin of a store where we shed our pennies for nigger-babies and tasteless, mottoed hearts. For after a few weeks, when it became clear that her cringing, mucoused talk was getting worse, she was transferred to the "ungraded" class. This group, made up of the mute, the shambling, and the oddly tall, some of whom were delivered by bus, was housed in a basement part of the school, with a separate entrance which was forbidden us not only by rule but by a lurking distaste of our own.

The year Mooley reappeared in Miss Totten's room, a dispute in the school system had disbanded all the ungraded classes in the city. Here and there, now, in the back seat of a class, there would be some grown-size boy who read haltingly from a primer, fingering the stubble on his slack jaw. Down in 4-A there was a shiny, petted doll of a girl, all crackling hairbow and nimble wheelchair, over whom the teachers shook their heads feelingly, saying: "Bright as a dollar! Imagine!" as if there were something sinister in the fact that useless legs had not impaired the musculature of a mind. And in our class, in harshly clean, faded dresses which were always a little too infantile for her, her spraying ginger hair cut short now and held by a round comb which circled the back of her head like a snaggle-toothed tiara which had slipped, there was this bony, bug-eyed wraith of a girl who raised her hand instead of saying "Present!" when Miss Totten said "Lilly Davis?" at roll call, and never spoke at all.

It was Juliet Hoffman, the pace-setter among the girls in the class, who spoke Mooley's nickname first. A jeweller's daughter, Juliet had achieved an eminence even beyond that due her curly profile, embroidered dresses, and prancing, leading-lady ways when, the Christmas before, she had brought as her present to teacher a real diamond ring. It had been a modest diamond, to be sure, but undoubtedly real, and set in real gold. Juliet had heralded it for weeks before and we had all seen it — it and the peculiar look on the face of the teacher, a young substitute whom we hardly knew — when she had lifted it from the pile of hankies and fancy notepaper on her desk. The teacher, over the syrupy protests of Mrs. Hoffman, had returned the ring, but its sparkle lingered on, iridescent around Juliet's head.

On our way out at three o'clock that first day with Miss Totten, Juliet nudged at me to wait. Obediently, I waited behind her. Twiddling her bunny muff, she minced over to the clothes closet and confronted the new girl.

"I know you," she said. "Mooley Davis, that's who you are!" A couple of the other children hung back to watch.

"Aren't you? Aren't you Mooley Davis?"

I remember just how Mooley stood there because of the coat she wore. She just stood there holding her coat against her stomach with both hands. It was a coat of some pale, vague tweed, cut the same length as mine. But it wrapped the wrong way over for a girl and the revers, wide ones, came all the way down and ended way below the pressing hands.

"Where you been?" Juliet flipped us all a knowing grin. "You been in ungraded?"

One of Mooley's shoulders inched up so that it almost touched her ear, but beyond that, she did not seem able to move. Her eyes looked at us, wide and fixed. I had the feeling that all of her had retreated far, far back behind the eyes which — large and light, and purposefully empty — had been forced to stay.

My back was to the room, but on the suddenly wooden faces of the others I saw Miss Totten's shadow. Then she loomed thinly over Juliet, her arms, which were crossed at her chest, hiding the one V of white in her garments, so that she looked like an umbrella which had been tightly furled.

"What's *your* name?" she asked, addressing not so much Juliet as the white muff which, I noticed now, was slightly soiled.

"Jooly-ette."

"Hmm. Oh, yes. Juliet Hoffman."

"Jooly-ette, it is." She pouted creamily up at Miss Totten, her glance narrow with the assurance of finger rings to come.

Something flickered in the nexus of yellow wrinkles around Miss Totten's lips. Poking out a bony forefinger, she held it against the muff. "You tell your mother," she said slowly, "that the way she spells it, it's *Juliet*."

Then she dismissed the rest of us but put a delaying hand on Mooley. Turning back to look, I saw that she had knelt down painfully, her skirt-hem graying in the floor dust, and staring absently over Mooley's head she was buttoning up the queerly shaped coat.

After a short, avid flurry of speculation we soon lost interest in Mooley, and in the routine Miss Totten devised for her. At first, during any kind of oral work, Mooley took her place at the blackboard and wrote down her answers, but later, Miss Totten sat her in the front row and gave her a small slate. She grew very quick at answering, particularly in "mental arithmetic" and in the card drills, when Miss Totten held up large Manila cards with significant locations and dates inscribed in her Palmer script, and we went down the rows, snapping back the answers.

Also, Mooley had acquired a protector in Ruby Green, the other Negro girl in the class — a huge, black girl with an arm-flailing, hee-haw way of talking and a rich, contralto singing voice which we had often heard in solo at Assembly. Ruby, boasting of her singing in night clubs on Saturday nights, of a father who had done time, cowed us all with these pungent inklings of the world on the other side of the dividing line of Amsterdam Avenue — that deep, velvet murk of Harlem which she lit for us with the flash of razors, the honky-tonk beat of the "numbahs," and the plangent wails of the mugged. Once, hearing David Hecker, a doctor's son, declare "Mooley has a cleft palate, that's what," Ruby wheeled and put a large hand on his shoulder, holding it there in menacing caress.

"She ain' got no cleff palate, see? She talk sometime, 'roun' home." She glared at us each in turn with such a pug-scowl that we flinched, thinking she was going to spit. Ruby giggled.

"She got no cause to talk, 'roun' here. She just don' need to bother." She lifted her hand from David, spinning him backward, and joined arms with the silent Mooley. "Me neither!" she added, and walked Mooley away, flinging back at us her gaudy, syncopated laugh.

Then one day, lolloping home after three, I suddenly remembered my books and tam, and above all my homework assignment, left in the pocket of my desk at school. I raced back there. The janitor, grumbling, unlocked the side door at which he had been sweeping and let me in. In the mauve, settling light the long maw of the gym held a rank, uneasy stillness. I walked up the spiral metal stairs feeling that I thieved on some part of the school's existence not intended for me. Outside the ambushed quiet of Miss Totten's room I stopped, gathering breath. Then I heard voices, one of them surely Miss Totten's dark, firm tones, the other no more than an arrested gurgle and pause.

I opened the door slowly. Miss Totten and Mooley raised their heads. It was odd, but although Miss Totten sat as usual at her desk, her hands clasped to one side of her hat, lunch-box, and the crinkly boa she wore all spring, and although Mooley was at her own desk in front of a spread copy of our thick reader, I felt the distinct, startled guilt of someone who interrupts an embrace.

"Yes?" said Miss Totten. Her eyes had the drugged look of eyes raised suddenly from close work. I fancied that she reddened slightly, like someone accused.

"I left my books."

Miss Totten nodded, and sat waiting. I walked down the row to my desk and bent over, fumbling for my things, my haunches awkward under the watchfulness behind me. At the door, with my arms full, I stopped, parroting the formula of dismissal.

"Good afternoon, Miss Totten."

"Good afternoon."

I walked home slowly. Miss Totten, when I spoke to her,

had seemed to be watching my mouth, almost with enmity. And in front of Mooley there had been no slate.

In class the next morning, as I collected the homework in my capacity as monitor, I lingered a minute at Mooley's desk, expecting some change, perhaps in her notice of me, but there was none. Her paper was the same as usual, written in a neat script quite legible in itself, but in a spidery back-hand which just faintly silvered the page, like a communiqué issued out of necessity, but begrudged.

Once more I had a glimpse of Miss Totten and Mooley together, on a day when I had joined the slangy, athletic Miss Steele who was striding capably along in her Ground Grippers on the route I usually took home. Almost at once I had known I was unwelcome, but I trotted desperately in her wake, not knowing how to relieve her of my company. At last a stitch in my side forced me to stop, in front of a corner fishmongers'.

"Folks who want to walk home with me have to step on it!" said Miss Steele. She allotted me one measuring, stone-blue glance, and moved on.

Disposed on the bald white window stall of the fish store there was a rigidly mounted eel which looked as if only its stuffing prevented it from growing onward, sinuously, from either impersonal end. Beside it were several tawny shells. A finger would have to avoid the spines on them before being able to touch their rosy, pursed throats. As the pain in my side lessened, I raised my head and saw my own face in the window, egg-shaped and sad. I turned away. Miss Totten and Mooley stood on the corner, their backs to me, waiting to cross. A trolley clanged by, then the street was clear, and

Miss Totten, looking down, nodded gently into the black boa and took Mooley by the hand. As they passed down the hill to St. Nicholas Avenue and disappeared, Mooley's face, smoothed out and grave, seemed to me, enviably, like the serene, guided faces of the children I had seen walking securely under the restful duennaship of nuns.

Then came the first day of Visiting Week, during which, according to convention, the normal school day would be on display, but for which we had actually been fortified with rapid-fire recitations which were supposed to erupt from us in sequence, like the somersaults which climax acrobatic acts. On this morning, just before we were called to order, Dr. Piatt, the principal, walked in. He was a gentle man, keeping to his office like a snail, and we had never succeeded in making a bogey of him, although we tried. Today he shepherded a group of mothers and two men, officiously dignified, all of whom he seated on some chairs up front at Miss Totten's left. Then he sat down too, looking upon us benignly, his head cocked a little to one side in a way he had, as if he hearkened to some unseen arbiter who whispered constantly to him of how bad children could be, but he benevolently, insistently, continued to disagree.

Miss Totten, alone among the teachers, was usually immune to visitors, but today she strode restlessly in front of us and as she pulled down the maps one of them slipped from her hand and snapped back up with a loud, flapping roar. Fumbling for the roll-book, she sat down and began to call the roll from it, something she usually did without looking at the book and favoring each of us, instead, with a warming nod.

"Arnold Ames?"

"Pres-unt!"

"Mary Bates?"

"Pres-unt!"

"Wanda Becovic?"

"Pres-unt!"

"Sidney Cohen?"

"Pres-unt!"

"L—Lilly Davis?"

It took us a minute to realize that Mooley had not raised her hand. A light, impatient groan rippled over the class. But Mooley, her face uplifted in a blank stare, was looking at Miss Totten. Miss Totten's own lips moved. There seemed to be a cord between her lips and Mooley's. Mooley's lips moved, opened.

"Pres-unt!" said Mooley.

The class caught its breath, then righted itself under the sweet, absent smile of the visitors. With flushed, lowered lids, but in a rich full voice, Miss Totten finished calling the roll. Then she rose and came forward with the Manila cards. Each time, she held up the name of a state and we answered with its capital city.

Pennsylvania.

"Harrisburg!" said Arnold Ames.

Illinois.

"Springfield!" said Mary Bates.

Arkansas.

"Little Rock!" said Wanda Becovic.

North Dakota.

"Bismark!" said Sidney Cohen.

Idaho.

We were afraid to turn our heads.

"Buh . . . Boise!" said Mooley Davis.

After this, we could hardly wait for the turn to come around to Mooley. When Miss Totten, using a pointer against the map, indicated that Mooley was to "bound" the state of North Carolina, we focused on one spot with such attention that the visitors, grinning at each other, shook their heads at such zest. But Dr. Piatt was looking straight at Miss Totten, his lips parted, his head no longer to one side.

"N-north Cal . . . Callina." Just as the deaf gaze at the speaking, Mooley's eyes never left Miss Totten's. Her voice issued, burred here, choked there, but unmistakably a voice. "Bounded by Virginia on the north . . . Tennessee on the west . . . South Callina on the south . . . and on the east . . . and on the east . . ." She bent her head and gripped her desk with her hands. I gripped my own desk, until I saw that she suffered only from the common failing — she had only forgotten. She raised her head.

"And on the east," she said joyously, "and on the east by the Atlannic Ocean."

Later that term Miss Totten died. She had been forty years in the school system, we heard in the eulogy at Assembly. There was no immediate family, and any of us who cared to might pay our respects at the chapel. After this, Mr. Moloney, who usually chose *Whispering* for the dismissal march, played something slow and thrumming which forced us to drag our feet until we reached the door.

Of course none of us went to the chapel, nor did any of us bother to wonder whether Mooley went. Probably she did not. For now that the girl withdrawn for so long behind those rigidly empty eyes had stepped forward into them, they flicked about quite normally, as captious as anyone's.

Once or twice in the days that followed we mentioned Miss Totten, but it was really death that we honored, clicking our tongues like our elders. Passing the umbrella-stand at home, I sometimes thought of Miss Totten, furled forever in her coffin. Then I forgot her too, along with the rest of the class. After all this was only reasonable in a class which had achieved Miss Steele.

But memory, after a time, dispenses its own emphasis, making a *feuilleton* of what we once thought most ponderable, laying its wreath on what we never thought to recall. In the country, the children stumble upon the griffin mask of the mangled pheasant, and they learn; they come upon the murderous love-knot of the mantis, and they surmise. But in the city, although no man looms very large against the sky, he is silhouetted all the more sharply against his fellows. And sometimes the children there, who know so little about the natural world, stumble still upon that unsolicited good which is perhaps only a dislocation in the insensitive rhythm of the natural world. And if they are lucky, memory holds it in waiting. For what they have stumbled upon is their own humanity — their aberration, and their glory. That must be why I find myself wanting to say aloud to someone: "I remember . . . a Miss Elizabeth Totten."

Letitia, Emeritus

HOLDING the small white card so as not to bend it, Letitia Reynolds Whyte, aged twenty-four, looked cautiously up and down the main hallway of the school. Only the Senior girls were left in the school now, and most of them were in their rooms, lying on the beds in their underwear, talking dreamily of what they were going to do after graduation, the ones who were not getting married, who were only going to Europe with their parents, or just back to Locust Valley, or Silver Spring, or Charleston, listening enviously to the fluttery, conscious plans of those who were. Through the closed door of the Green Room down at the end of the hall she heard the laughter of the girls closeted there, rehearsing the skits for the Senior Banquet that evening. Tomorrow, hordes of parents would descend on the school for the graduation exercises, but today, the empty lawns outside — carefully shaven to a final unusual neatness that morning by Norval, the gardener — the echoing halls inside, all had a hush over them, a left behind hush of desertions and departures, of feverish routines suspended, of another school year gone, and another deadened summer begun, in which only Miss Sopes — the Head — the colored cook, and Norval would be left to wait for fall. And, of course, Letitia.

She looked up and down the hall again. All the teachers' cubbyhole private offices were closed and locked, even the larger one at the very end, a former parlor, which was rated by "Papa Davis," Professor Walter Wallace Davis, because he was the oldest, the most distinguished looking, and the only one who was a real professor, having come to Hyacinth Hall after the close of a career in Latin and Greek at the State University. Usually, long after the others had locked up and gone he could be found lingering in the musty brown room with the shabby davenport and the bronze lamp with the purple frosted grapes. "This is my real home, girls. My real home," he would say, leaning forward and smiling expansively, rubbing the grapes with a restless, worrying hand. But today even he had gone home to his palsied sister in their dark old house across the bridge in Minetteville, although he would return tomorrow to address the parents, as he did every year at graduation.

Satisfied that no one was around, Letitia crossed the hall to the large Student Mail box which hung on the wall in its very center. Ordinarily the box was a plain drab, lettered "Hyacinth Hall" in white, a smart, monogram-like inscription which the elder, dead Miss Sopes, *the* Miss Sopes, in some fierce spinsterish urge, thwarted possibly as to bedspreads and guest towels, had always had imprinted on every wastebasket, towel, door, and object that attached to the Hall. This tradition, like every one which stemmed from the mourned competence of her sister, the present tremulous Miss Rosanna had of course carried on.

Today, in accordance with still another tradition, the box
was covered, except for the slit for envelopes, with a large,
fanned-out frill of stiff white paper, and stuck above it, a
fancily inked sign said "Announcements." All week long
Senior girls had been surreptitiously seeking out the box and
dropping in their white cards, or slips of pink or blue notepaper, when no one was looking. On Banquet night, the
box, lifted from its hooks, would be set in the middle of
the draped head table where the class officers sat, and after
the jerkily rhymed class history had been read and the class
prophecies for each girl had sent them all into gales of
merriment, the class president, standing solemnly above the
box, would dip her hand into it slowly, teasingly, and read
off, one by one, the names and announcements of all the
girls who were leaving Hyacinth Hall "engaged." Each girl
stood, was clapped for, walked forward smiling and reddened to the head table and was handed a long-stemmed
rose, which she pinned to her shoulder and wore mincingly
the rest of the evening. A girl could not just put any name,
or even the name of her "steady" in the box. She had to be
really, seriously engaged. Letitia knew, for Senior Banquet,
since there were never any boys present, was one of the
school functions she was allowed to attend. She had been
to two of them already. Tonight's would be the third.

After one more hesitant look around, she bent over the
card in her hand, scrutinized it lovingly, tabbing each letter
with a slow forefinger. Some of the girls even got themselves engaged just so they could announce it on Banquet
night; just so they would not have to be one of the others
barred from the flushed group of those who had been tapped,

anointed, by love's mysterious rose. Just a few nights ago, Letitia, leaning pressed against the locked connecting side door of her room, the door which led to Willa Mae Fordyce's room on the other side, but was never opened, had heard Willa proclaiming to other murmurous visiting voices: "Why I'd count it a disgrace not to announce on Banquet night, really I would. I just wouldn't feel *graduated,* honest!" And Willa had given a low, satisfied laugh. She had meant it too, for just this morning, Letitia, stealing breathlessly into Willa's empty room through the unlocked regular door, had seen the slip readied on Willa's desk. "Engaged. Wilhelmina Mary Fordyce and Homer Watson Ames."

Letitia gave her own card a last admiring look. It was beautifully printed — the best she had ever done. In art class, Miss Tolliver would often pause, leaning over Letitia's shoulder, and knitting together tenderly her gray, mock-fierce eyebrows, she would say, extra-loud: " 'Titia, your copy-work is certainly real nice, dear. Truly lovely." And shaking her head at some imaginary crony in the air, she would make a kind of soft sad sigh and pass on to the desk of the girl in front.

Almost reluctantly, Letitia raised the hand with the card in it, held it poised near the paper frill for a second, then quickly pushed the card through the slit in the box. She heard the slight sound it made, not the sharp tap of paper falling into empty metal, but a slithery rustle which meant that it had fallen on others like it. She gave her flat, tuneless giggle, which always sounded as if it needed finishing, and turning away in the dogged, laborious way she had, she walked down the marble steps, out onto the lawn, and across it to the pretty gabled dormitory on the other side.

From behind, with her pale blonde hair swinging over the pink cashmere sweater and the dyed-to-match tweed skirt, with her loafers and pink socks, Letitia looked like any one of a dozen others. Even better groomed, even a little too carefully matched, perhaps — as she had been ever since that day, six years ago, when she had walked into her first class at the school, her mouth, which peaked way up in the center like a baby's, widened in a grin, on her head, perched clumsily there, the glittering gold sequin and seed-pearl cap which an inept uncle, knowing her fondness for shiny gauds, had given her for Christmas. Ever since then, Delia, the light-colored upstairs girl, who had seen service as a personal maid on some of the big estates near the school, had been detailed to go to Miss Letitia's room each morning and set out the proper clothes for the weather and the day. Sometimes, if there was a special occasion, although there seldom was, Delia came in the evening, too. In the summer, when Delia worked elsewhere, Miss Rosanna came herself, and would stand there clucking a little to herself, her unassertive manner sharpened with impatience, although once in a while she spent a little extra time handling greedily the beautiful quality underwear and clothes Letitia's family bought and sent down to her, with never any trouble about sizes or ideas, for the girl had stayed the same and looked the same as when she first came.

Even when people saw her from the front, saw the domed childish forehead, the eyes, large with a painful attention, the peaked fledgling mouth always open as if waiting for someone to push into it the blessed worm of enlightenment

— even then they were not sure. Feature by feature the face was a pretty one. It was only as people waited covertly for reflection to shadow the eyes, for a self to assemble and animate the face, that the doubt stole over them. The creeping realization began to form only as, shrinking, they became aware of the presence of that same straining of a blocked sense which they felt in the presence of the deaf who leaned to listen, the blind who stretched to feel. But when they heard the light, singsong rote of the voice, the sentence that petered into a laugh, the laugh that was like a pitch-pipe whose single note was query — then they were sure.

Then it was that, at a tea where Mrs. Reese Reynolds Whyte poured, or at a meeting of which she was inevitably chairman, one or the other of the women would purr in the ear of her neighbor: "You've seen that youngest daughter of Gratia Whyte's . . . is she quite . . . ?" and the other would answer: "All right . . . you mean? . . ." covering the words with a disclaiming shrug.

"Borderline?" This, avidly, from the inquirer.

"Well . . . you know Gratia . . ." might come the discreet answer. "She can face up to anything. . . . Look at how they drag the father with them . . . lectures, everywhere!"

It was through the means of Hyacinth Hall that Mrs. Whyte had faced up to Letitia. The Whytes belonged to those quiet rich who managed to imply, by their abstention from show, their endorsement of the proper, noncontroversial causes, such as Poetry and Peace, that wealth could be noble and remain fruitfully in the hands of its rightful inheritors. Summer and winter, their homes had a serene dowdiness possible only to those who could afford to be contemptuous of fashion. Their limousines were the heaviest, but dark, their servants and appurtenances of the most durable best, and none of these was changed too often. Mrs. Whyte had not only "attended" but graduated from one of the severer colleges long before it became commonplace for debutantes to do so, and from the list of benefactions which offered opportunities for conspicuous waste in an altruistic form, she had long since dropped the sponsorship of day nurseries and fallen women, leaving this to the less intellectual members of Society. It was in the poetry leagues and the English-speaking unions that she could be found, and in those spontaneous, pacifist groups of women which were most fervid and vocal just before a war, were as swiftly transmuted into "Bundles for Something" during the war's course, and were once again transformed by victory into Leagues for a Proper Peace. It was related of her, and justly, that she had downed in debate (at a benefit) a Justice of the Supreme Court (retired). Her three daughters before Letitia, had been sent, not to Miss Hewitt's Classes, or various "Halls" in America or Lausanne, but to Radcliffe, Bryn Mawr, and in one case, Oxford, after which, their doughy faces veiled by Venus-nets of trust funds, they had achieved marriage, and settled down to inheriting their mother's committeeships.

Therefore, when Hyacinth Hall, in straits after the death of its founder, had circulated an appeal to "its friends" to rally and save it, it had not been likely that Mrs. Whyte would appear in that category, since the school was superannuated, of a type she deplored, and located beyond the

Eastern seaboard, in a part of America in whose pretenses she did not acquiesce. As for Letitia, she had long since been taught at home by elderly women whose need made them tactful, whose chief function was to maintain the tacit assumption that she was being taught at all.

On the very day, however, that Mrs. Whyte received the letter from the Hall in her morning mail, the housekeeper had appeared in her sitting-room, red-faced, almost in tears, with the tale that Miss Letitia was bothering the houseman again.

After the housekeeper had been reassured, halted just short of a bosomy, sisterly commiseration Mrs. Whyte could not have tolerated either as a woman or as an employer, Letitia's mother sat over her dilemma for a long time, contemplating the pitiful mauraudings of her innocent. Then, with one of those masterly inspirations which had made her such a jewel among committeewomen, she had riffled hastily through her correspondence for the letter from the Hall. The school, she recalled, was situated in fox-hunting country; its girls spent a good part of their time in riding clothes. And Letitia could ride, had even appeared unobtrusively, years ago, at one or two shows, in the children's class. She had proved unequal to jumping, or anything fancy; she required a gentle mount, but she loved horses, and she could ride. Her sole other talent, that for "art work," would certainly find a place in the rudimentary classes of such a school, or else one of those special arrangements, of which she had already had so many in her life, could always be made. And what better place for protection, for segregation without emphasis, than a girl's school, especially one where, its highest aim being to equip its young ladies with all the attractions and accoutrements of the belle, the value of protection was understood better than any other?

Therefore, on the list of the influential few who had rallied to the support of the Hall, none had rallied harder than Mrs. Whyte. And at the end of that summer six years before, the newspaper of the little Hudson River town where the Whytes had their bracketed gothic summer place, had reported: "Mr and Mrs. Reese Reynolds Whyte and their daughter, Miss Letitia Reynolds Whyte, have left for an extended motor tour of the South, their destination Hya-- cinth Hall, the well-known finishing school, where Miss Whyte will enroll as an art student. Accompanying them is their house guest, Dame Alice Mellish, recently honored by His Majesty, the King of England, for her studies in Anglo-American semantics."

It had been a queer entourage which had descended upon the school in those last deciduous days of summer. The few teachers and students already there, waiting out the close, inert days before the beginning of the term, were energized and impressed by the visitors, whose confident eccentricity had as surely betokened superiority. Flanked by Mrs. Whyte, a type instantly recognizable and acceptable, and by Dame Alice, whose skirts were uneven to the point of vagary, but whose title had preceded her through the school like an odor, had come Letitia, not so instantly recognizable, but soon to be. And wheeled out, in dark finale, from the capacious back of the car, had come the chair bearing Mr. Whyte, a beautifully groomed old man in lawyer's black and a stiff collar, his very clean hands nerveless on his knees, the fixed upward twist of one side of his mouth lending him a demeanor of unchangeable pleasure. He did not talk, and apparently could not, but his lack, appearing at the end of life rather than at the beginning, was an honorable one which needed not to be hidden, and he was wheeled in and out of every conversation. From time to time, the chauffeur who attended him leaned over and removed or replaced the silky black beaver hat on the silver head at the proper intervals, and this, seeming to be done according to some prescribed rhythm of etiquette, not only lent the old man a verisimilitude of activity, but created, also, an atmosphere of the most recherché good taste. And when Mrs. Whyte, pointing her arches carefully before her, trailing the confused and conquered Miss Rosanna behind her, had clacked down the marble steps of the main building, she had sailed right up to the wheel chair, which had not attempted the steps, as to a reviewing stand, and with nods and becks and the most wreathed of smiles, had apparently recounted the whole transaction to the unchangeable benevolence of Father.

The Whytes did not stay the night at the school. They departed that same evening, leaving behind them a legend, that had faded, and Letitia, who had stayed the same.

So it was that Letitia, entering her hot, still room on this particular day, entered the only permanent room in the dormitory, a room from which she yearned, each expectant June, to be delivered, and to which she was, each disappointed June, remanded. Most of the other rooms had a littered, bird-of-passage look which suggested that the girl in each was only sojourning on her way to wider fields which Letitia, while she craved them, could not have described. Letitia's room, however, had the same supervised neatness as her person, and with its pictures of her family hanging on the wall in circular silver frames, its chiming clock near the bed, and its large calendar with the block numbers marked off crosswise, looked as if it had long ago made its concessions to forever. During one or two of the early years, the accident of a friendly girl neighbor next door had permitted the unlocking of the connecting door between the rooms, as was done everywhere else in the school, but with the coming of Willa Mae, all this had changed, and little by little, Letitia's almost tolerated, almost earned place in the humming, cozy undercurrents of the dormitory, had slipped away.

"Honestly, Mum," Willa had reported at home, "it would give you the creeps! Really it would!" And at the very next Parents' Day, Mrs. Fordyce, not having trusted herself among the delicacies of correspondence, had actually broached the subject, gaspingly, to Miss Rosanna, but had found her, under her cloud of faltering reassurances, unexpectedly immovable. For the special arrangement for Letitia was large.

Nevertheless, the last four years had come to have a painful weight of their own, had come to be known, in her sharded thoughts, as "the locked-door years." But now, as she closed the door behind her, excitement twitched at her mouth, gave almost a complexity to the clear glass of her eyes. For a minute she stood in the room like a stranger to it, as if waiting for someone to tell her what to do next. Then she went to the dresser and pulled out a drawer. Behind a pile of tailored slips, all alike, which she moved to one side with patient tidiness, she found what she wanted. With a crow of pleasure, she drew out the sequinned cap and held it in her hand. Straightening up, she walked over to the window, hung the cap on the hooked ornament at the end of the window-shade cord, and stood there dazzled, watching it.

Until now, there had been no occasion important enough for it since the fiasco of its first wearing. Early in her first year at the school Letitia had been permitted to attend the initial one of the highly chaperoned dances which occurred there several times a year in co-operation with a nearby military academy. Halfway through the evening, an af-frighted young man, flying incontinently from the coat room, and an incredulous wave of gossip, rippling through the dancers, had made it all too apparent that either Mrs. Whyte's strictures to Miss Rosanna had been too reserved, or Miss Rosanna's interpretation of them insufficiently literal. Ever since then, on such evenings, Letitia, accompanied by Delia, had been sent to the movies in Minetteville, where they stayed right through the double feature, and often even sat over a sundae at Whalen's afterwards, although Delia, admitted there in her capacity as duenna, never ate anything, but sat stiffly, referring quietly from time to time to the watch the Whytes had sent her after the first year.

Now, twisting and turning with a purposeful motion of its own, the cap dangled and reversed itself, glittering in the sun. A prism of light, deflected from it, kindled the silver frames of the pictures, where they hung on the wall, dis-regarded by Letitia's glance, as their originals hung, neg-

lected, in the dusty galleries of her remembrance. Twice a
year she saw her family briefly, but so briefly, so remotely
across the hedge to another world, that they had all but
receded into symbols of that larger existence into which one
was accepted, to which one acceded only after the mystical
rite of graduation.

All the signposts, all the clues, had brought Letitia around
to this conclusion, and helped by circumstance, to her con-
trivance for escape. On the door of Papa Davis' office, a
yellowed card, pinned to the aged door frame, said in
gothicked lettering: "Walter Wallace Davis. Professor,
Emeritus," and only yesterday, straying in there in answer
to his eager, scooping glance, she had stopped to peer
closer, almost professionally, at the lettering on the card,
and with a delaying finger on the last queer word, had asked
its meaning. Papa Davis had risen from his arm chair and
bent closer to her over the card, as if he too had had to
ponder its meaning. Then, tossing back his head so that she
had seen the waggle-tuft of beard on his chin pointing
straight out, he had laughed in his neighing voice.

"Graduated!" he had said, smiling at her, nodding like a
pendulum. "It means 'graduated,'" he had added, frowning.
"Leaving a place forever." In the silence that fell between
them he had kept on speculatively nodding. He had stretched
an arm past her, then, to grasp the door, had leaned out to
stare fretfully up and down the empty corridor, and stepping
back into the room, had softly closed the door and locked
it.

Even when he had come closer, very close, she had been
unalarmed. Each year the school put on a Roman Festival,

and Papa Davis had been present at rehearsals to hear the Latin declamations, and pass on the authenticity of the home-draped togas. If she had seen the girls exploding into silent laughter in a corner, if she had heard one whispering to another "Papa Davis has to feel you to see if you're Roman!" it had meant to her, perhaps, one more cryptic notion of authority, or perhaps nothing at all. And so, if at first she had watched his overtures with a docility heightened only with curiosity, then later she had received them with eager warmth, even though he was nothing like the young men to whom she had once put out a questing hand. For the force of his words, just said, hung around him like a clue, a means to an end. Then, too, she had heard him say so often in his peevish, solitary voice, that the school was his real, his only home, and this, interpreted as a complaint, had harped on a reality she understood, which made them kin. And finally, gazing up at him from the cracked leather davenport, she had seen that, with his avid lip drawn back over the long yellow teeth, he had looked unintimidating, familiar, like an old, begging horse.

Now she lifted the cap away from the window, twirled it several times over in her fingers, and walked over to the mirror. With a single uncalculated movement she put the cap on her head and looked into the mirror with a pleased smile. Then she walked over to her desk. Strewn over its surface were a number of small white cards, discarded trial copies of that final, faultless one she had put in the school mail-box.

Still holding the sparkling cap awkwardly to her head with one hand, she bent over the desk and picked up one of the cards. Beautifully printed and shaded in India ink, it seemed unmarred, and in truth, working delightedly all that morning over her inscriptions, she had been almost reluctant to settle on one as perfect enough for her vivid purpose. She had copied the first word secretly from the slip on Willa Mae's desk. Her own name she knew how to do. The last of the legend she had transcribed lovingly from the yellowed card rifled from Professor Davis' office door. Only, here, with this last, making a single change which for her amounted to an act of creation, almost of intelligence, she had inverted the sequence, so that the little card she held in her hand now, copy of that still more perfect one she had slipped into the box, read:

"Engaged. Professor Walter Wallace Davis. And Letitia Reynolds Whyte, Emeritus."

Night Riders of Northville

On smoky spring evenings, from the windows of the commuter's train which rides through the lowlands of Jersey, the little bars, which are seldom more than a block or so from the stations, look like hot coals burning in the thin dusk. Spotted over the countryside, they send up their signal flares, promising the fought-off moment of excitement before you open the door — when it seems as if someone may just this minute have said: "Here is the place — *the place*," and the flat, sold feeling after the door is open, and you see that this is just about like any such place anywhere.

If, having missed your usual train perhaps, you stop off at the particular hole-in-a-corner which clings to your station — Joe's Place, or Morelli's, or the Rainbow Tavern — and you sit there over your glass, after your phone call, waiting for the taxi or the wife with the car — then you may find, after the quick rash of one-shot commuters is over, that you are alone, or almost alone, with perhaps a solitary, leather-jacketed baggageman musing over his beer on his stool down at the other end. And you wonder what keeps a joint like this alive.

Down in the thriving center of town, or settled here and there on its skirting streets, are places, certainly, which cater more specially to a man's sudden convivial needs, or to his malaises. Out on the highway which is never far from such a town, the roadhouses, each evening, corral the people who want steak, pizza, chicken-in-the-basket. There is a "good place to take the family and still get a drink," a haunt for the juke-box babies, a daytime spot which draws the lawyers from the courthouse over at the county seat, even a swank little box of a place where certain rich women of the town gather to sip away time from the huge carafe of it that confronts them each day between breakfast and the arrival of the evening train. And because no man or woman lives his life in just one context, sooner or later you may see a person who more properly belongs in a particular one of these places, seated, explicably or not, in another.

But the nondescript place where you are sitting now — could it be said to have a category? To whom or what could it cater, other than to the casual, modestly sated thirsts of its portion of two trainfuls a day of men homeward bound toward the snow shovel or the garden, or toward the less seasonal dictates of the television, the wife, and the children with egg on their chins? And as you rise, relievedly, to the toot of a horn outside, and exchange diffident nods with the owner, you decide that his reserve with you on this and other occasions is the case, not because you are not a regular, but because there are no regulars here. As you go out the door, you wonder idly how he hangs on here at all, and you imagine him of a Sunday, when the trains are all but stilled, totting up his supplier's bills and his receipts, and worrying about a better spot for trade.

Should you sit on there for a sufficient number of evenings, however, you might learn how wrong you were. For that place is one of a circuit of such places which certain men of the town ride ceaselessly, for reasons which neither appear to be simple nor are.

Take, for instance, the Rainbow Tavern at Northville, and four of its regulars — James De Vries, Dicky English, Jack Burdette, and Henry Lister. If you get to know the habits of these four, who are sure to appear there singly or in varying combinations almost every night of the week — and if you also happen to learn of a minor tragedy which befell one of them — then in the course of time you may also sense, although you may never quite be able to put your finger on it, the nature of that *spécialité de la maison* which is served by the Rainbow Tavern.

James De Vries, who is always called "the judge," out of deference to the fact that he was once, for several years, a justice of the peace, is the only one of the four who was born in Northville — and perhaps some of the deference is to this fact too. In a town where most of the men make their living elsewhere, he is one of those vanishing few who subsist on their inherited knowledge of the place and the "connections" in it — a little banking, some law, a few real estate transactions, and a little politicking. He can tell you the real legend of the old Viner place, and what went on there in the old days, can search a title in his mind before he has to refer to county records, and lives in the ground-floor apartment of the cupolaed house in which he was born — the house bought by his grandfather, who was a minor henchman of Boss Tweed. Although there has never been any suggestion of financial hanky-panky about his own reputation, there still clings to him, somehow, the equivocal aura of the man who turns a dollar because he is in the know. As he stands at the bar, with his hat brim turned low over his long, swart face, so that if you are near him and fairly tall you cannot glimpse anything but his mouth (for the judge is quite short, and in the manner of many short men, affects hats a little too high in the crown and wide of brim), he keeps a silence weighted faintly with an indication that silence is what he has come here for. If he is addressed, however, on a question of local affairs, he likes to pronounce the answers in a measured, monotonous voice, although he will never keep the conversational ball rolling with the added fillip of a question or an opinion. He is at the bar briefly at five, at seven-thirty, and at ten, so precisely that Denis, the owner, often may answer a time query from one of the regulars: "Almost time for the judge's last round." He has two drinks at five, three at seven-thirty, and three at ten, always of straight bourbon with a dash of bitters, and always set before him by Denis as soon as he appears. He has probably not ordered out loud for years, never buys or is bought a drink, and has long since managed to convey, by this routine, that for him, liquor — something to be accomplished, as it were, as is a meal by a man not interested in the table — is never in any case a specific for some disreputable need. It is ironic, therefore, that in a place where casualness and haphazard spontaneity are part of the mores, the very carefulness of the judge's behavior has made him the oddity he imagines he is not.

For, often, when a man is to be found night after night in the same place, swaying deep in drink, progressing through the stereotype stages of the drunk — from the painful interest in each newcomer, the mumbled revelation to the bartender, down to the final, locked communion with the glass — often a common thing to be heard in the pitying undertones behind him is: "Nice guy though. They say his wife is a bitch." But in the Rainbow Tavern this is most commonly said of the judge. Not by any of the other three regulars, incidentally, for all the regulars share a solidarity of reticence about their affairs outside, one even stronger than is usual among men, perhaps, and peculiarly noticeable, since it suggests that, with them, home may be really the outside, and "inside" is here. No one knows the origin of this rumor about the judge, or any verification for it, for although the other three know each other in another context, the social life of the town — have visited each other in their homes, and even, by prearrangement, have brought their wives here, after the manner of men who twice a year tolerate ladies' night at the club — the judge does not know any of these people socially, and never brings his "outside" here. The rumor arises, possibly, because there is no worse place to hide than among the heightened awareness of others who are hiding too.

When a man walks into the Rainbow Tavern, it is often possible to tell his mood, at what stage in the circuit he is, or how full he is or intends to be, from the angle at which he wears his hat. Dicky English's hat is always tipped toward the back of his head. This is true of him wherever he is making an entrance, whether to the Rainbow or others of its ilk, to a party, to a meeting of one of the dozens of committees on which he is a prime mover, or to the smoker of the morning train. A buzzing, bustling, smart dresser of a man, in whose freshly barbered face, above his bow-tie, the slightly juvenile features are only healthfully obscured by a faintly moony, fortyish fat, Dicky, if not exactly a dream of fair women, is conceivably that of a number of fair typists in the office of which he is manager. Only longer acquaintance with him suggests that in his very trueness to form there is something much too credible. Watching Dicky at first, one is bored or amused by the larger-than-life verisimilitude of the man; later one wonders how, under such a bewildering collection of verisimilitudes, there can be a man at all. Here, one says, as he struts chestily into a conversation, or, his backside waggling in jaunty efficiency, is seen disappearing round the bend in the center of two or three cronies he has marshalled on an errand of pleasure — here is the eternal seller of tickets to raffles, the organizer of poker games and pig roasts; here is the life-of-the-party, in whom, as with so many such, there is just enough of the clown, the simpleton, the butt — so that by his very *bêtises* he breaks down the united ice of others, warming them, even at the cost of ridicule, to that sense of occasion he craves.

To his intimates at the Rainbow, where his invariable greeting is "You're planning to go, aren't you?" his invariable adieu "Be sure to be there, now," Dicky passes for a joiner, a mixer, a man whose compulsion barely escapes buffoonery, but is invaluable to those whose gregariousness is more wistful, less competent. He is sensitive to the needs of the company, too — a Rotarian in Rotary, a father among fathers, a fornicator among fornicators — always so long as he can go on talking. Even his drinking is versatile and somehow controlled; he is good for an elegiac, gossipy chat in a corner or for an all-night spree with the boys, but even in the midst of the spree he never seems *personally* drunk. Only when you see him at home, a paterfamilias outdoing all others, or at a roadhouse, perhaps, this time with the wife, to whom he is playing the uxoriously gallant part of the husband on his girl's night out, or in the morning smoker, where he persists in reading tidbits of news to men whose issues of the same paper are already slack and crumpled in their hands — only then may you realize that Dicky is more than a man who lives for the occasion — he is a man who cannot live without it, however small. Like those little mechanical toy men with the keys in their split, metal backs, he will scuttle around and around only as long as the original impetus lasts — one begins to imagine, behind the truckling rounds of his talk, a gasping prescience that, when he slackens, he will topple over on his side forever. He is a man who convinces himself into humanity only by the ululating sound of his own voice. And because one can imagine him en route to an experience, or possibly from it, but never actually in the middle of it, one can form conclusions as to Dicky's reasons for stopping so often at a place like the Rainbow, which is essentially, after all, en route.

As for Jack Burdette and Henry Lister, there is no need to

take up separately two who are almost always together. They roomed together at college, went into business and married at about the same time, bought houses on adjoining streets in that fancy modern development in Northville before it was too evident that their wives would never get along, and refugees now, each from the disapproval of two wives, are ever more closely united in the deep beatitudes of the bottle. Jack is a great beef of a man with a fine nose only just beginning to vein, and an extraordinarily sweet smile which, with the cleft in the first of his chins, forms a solitary fleur-de-lys above the others. He is one of those large, deceptively solid men who melt in drink: as the evening advances, the smile grows fixed on a face which recedes behind it like a huge, fair egg, the bottom outline of which has been drawn several times over by a wavering artist.

Seen over his shoulder, in that rich, Rembrandt-colored air of the Rainbow, which is half submerged smell, half expunged light, Henry Lister's face, mouse-sharp and precise, does not change at all. There is no mystery about Henry unless it is the absence of one. He is a neutral, common denominator of a man, whose only departure from the ordinary is his drinking; even the latter seems an effort to fill up the uncomfortable reservoir of his averageness. He is never out of place in any company he keeps, and never quite of it; he is a man who is always seen over someone else's shoulder — in this case Jack's.

Over the years, the association of these two has effected a likeness quite apart from looks — the kind of dual semblance which occurs in a long, uneventful marriage. Jack, who is an investment counselor, often surprises his business acquaintances with quite a bookish allusion, and Henry, who is in the trade department of a publishing house, is considered by his colleagues to be pretty sharp on the market. During the business day, Jack's eye is remarkably clear and shrewd, notwithstanding the night before, and Henry's manner may be a little on the vague side, but at closing time in the Rainbow, after the long, matched session of glass for glass, it is Henry who gently leads the faltering Jack away from the bar and drives him home.

One might think that their wives — both childless, both graduates of the stern discipline of the evasive phone call, the mummified supper, the endless evening in the empty living room, of which there happens to be a counterpart not half a block away — one would think that they might pool their grievances in a sort of friendship too. Such is not the case, however. They hate each other — oddly enough each of the women saves her invective not for her rival, but for his wife. It is simpler that way perhaps. Or possibly it is easier to bear the onus of a rival than the presence of someone whose grievances are the same.

Once or twice Henry and Jack have been known to josh each other over this quirk of Alice's and Mary Lou's, but only in the clichés with which men refer to women at the Rainbow, where it is generally conceded that the ladies, all of them sphinxes, are worth the solving at times, but blessedly not here and now. Mostly, however, the two men sit on in silence, accumulating on the abacus of their bar bill an ever huger total of hours they have spent thus together, two eunuchs sitting in a quietude from which trouble has been castrated, at a comfortable, derisive distance from the harem.

This, then, was the way things stood with the four regulars, when Mrs. Henry Lister, on a pink May evening which contrasted, who knows how fiercely, with her sallow day, cut her wrists.

On this particular Monday night, when the phone rang in the booth at the Rainbow, the four men had the bar to themselves. This is often the case on Mondays, for at the Rainbow there is a discernible, taken-for-granted rhythm to the evenings of the week. Sunday is the big night; Denis is rarely able to close the place until four. Tuesdays and Wednesdays are slow; even Henry and Jack may not appear until after ten or perhaps not at all, presumably having gone home for a token dinner and been prevailed upon to stay. Thursdays are pretty normal, and Fridays the bar begins to expand again, with men who drink in a certain propriety, duty-bound, as it were, to honor the inception of the week end. Saturday is a poor night for the regulars, who are shunted out of their niche by celebrants who come (as the four indicate to each other with faint shrugs) apparently from nowhere, and Denis is kept busy shooing minors out of the place. But on Sunday nights the bar really hums, with an added group of familiars who arrive gratefully after the dearth of the day. Meeting on the station platform the morning after, the three regulars (for the judge, of course, does not commute) greet each other with reminiscent shakes of the head, eying each other's gray gills and red, granular eyelids, and sit at an understanding distance from each other in the smoker, retiring glumly behind their papers. If a man just makes the train by the skin of his teeth, this is the one morning in which he is not chaffed. Even Dicky English has learned to shut his face on Monday mornings.

During this particular first day of the business week, the city streets had been stroked with summer. When the evening train set down its passengers in Northville, it could be seen that the leaves, although still new against the sky, were no longer single and choice. The air had a beautiful, clear expectancy about it, like the inside of a glass bell that was about to be rung. The door of the Rainbow, though not yet screened, had been ajar.

Now, with the bar to themselves, the four were settled restfully on their stools like convalescents from a mutual illness, just able to savor the malted dimness of the place in the safely muted company of their kind. Henry and Jack had been here since train time, the judge was in the middle of his second round, and Dicky had just breezed in.

"Some night last night, eh Denis?" said Dicky.

Denis nodded. He was a profound listener, with a repertoire of silent assent which ranged from the nod to a look of alert, pained sympathy which came, actually, from varicosed veins, but was a great help to his business.

Dicky tipped his hat further back on his head. "Hear Patterson's still on the town. They say he never did get home."

"In here about four o'clock for a minute," said Denis, polishing a glass.

"Better watch himself lately." Dicky clapped his hands together, raised one to readjust his hat, looked about him minutely as if to search the possibilities of the hour, and let his arm sink around Jack's neck. "Howja do at the office today pal?"

Jack turned his head carefully within the crook of the encircling arm, and smiled his sweet, ponderous smile. "I died," he said.

"How about Henry, there? He looks able to sit up and take nourishment?"

Henry screwed his eyes shut appreciatively, but made no answer. Down at the left end of the bar, the judge looked owlishly into an empty glass, Denis moved quickly to replace it with the third and last of his round. And the telephone rang.

No one at the bar flinched in notice, although the telephone rings infrequently at the Rainbow. The phone knew better than to call for any of the men here.

Denis shuffled through the archway into the alcove which held the phone booth and the pinball machine. After a minute he returned, gestured at Henry, and returned to his polishing. Henry pointed at himself with raised eyebrows, shrugged, and walked out to the booth. He was there for some time.

"Da-te-da, da-te-da, da-te-da," said Dicky, falsetto.

Jack hunched himself over the bar, lit a cigarette, dropped the match on the floor before it was quite dead, and rubbed it out with his shoe.

"Jesus Henry what's wrong?" said Dicky.

Henry stood in the archway, his face white, his arms dangling uncertainly at his sides. "The police. They took Alice to the hospital."

Jack lurched to his feet. "Something with the car, Hen?"

"She tried to . . ." Henry turned his head from side to side. "She acted all right this morning," he said on a high note. "She acted perfectly O.K."

"Drive you down, fella?" said Dicky.

Henry seemed not to have heard him. He reached out .nd touched the bar surface, moving his hand along as if he expected to find a tab there. "They want to type my blood they said." He moved toward the door.

"I'll go with you, Hen." Jack went toward him, weaving a little.

"No," said Henry. His eyes returned to focus. He shivered. "No. Don't do that, Jack." He went out the door.

"Call me here. Call me if you need me." There was no answer except the current of air from the swinging door. They heard the splutter of a motor, its outraged whine and diminuendo. Through the door, which remained ajar, came the dark, stealing scents of May. After a minute, Denis walked over and closed it.

"She have a miss, you think?" whispered Dicky. No one answered him.

The judge coughed, and spoke. "Sold them that house they have. Over on Summit. June '42 it was, just before the rise. Nice little property." He shook his head, as if he could not be responsible for the way people mishandled the lives to which he had helped them attach a property of value. Then, glancing at the clock, he saw that it was time. Pulling his hat brim lower, he nodded and left.

"Well, guess I'm on my way too," said Dicky. "Drop you, Jack? Well, see you in the morning then." He eased himself halfway out the door, then poked his head back in.

"Chilly," he said, shaking his head solemnly, and shut the door behind him.

It can be awkward, drinking alone at a bar. Is the man behind it wholly a servitor at such times, or must recognition be made of the fact that two human beings are together in an otherwise empty room? At such times it is good to be where one is known. Denis sat reading his newspaper, his shell-rims far down on his nose, his presence as sane and reassuring as a night nurse. It was a racing final he read; occasionally he made a mark on it with a pencil, or rose to freshen Jack's glass. There were no other demands on his attention either from his customer or from the phone. Gradually the room, although it had no fireplace, took on the guttered look of a room in which a fire has died down. When the late freight chuffed by on her way to Newburgh, Denis went to the booth, called a cabby with whom he had an arrangement, shook Jack by the shoulder, and sent him home.

The next day, Dicky English, purveying the news to the smoker, had the field to himself. Henry, of course, was absent, and Jack did not appear for several days. On the second of these, the smoker heard, as the town had already heard, that Mrs. Henry Lister had muffed it. She would survive. This was received as such news is. The suicide attempt which is successful has an awesome achievement about it, before which we quail, but bow. It is a terrible epitaph, but it is one, and its headstone will sooner or later be obscured like any other. But the incompetent who has botched, who has been retrieved against his will, has committed an indecency. He has brought his nakedness not to the tomb, but to the tea table. Later, his existence will fret us like that of the invalid whose ailment death refuses to dignify.

On the morning when Jack returned to the train, it was observed that he had the drained, pearly look of dedication of the man who is on the wagon. No comments were made, since it was known how close Jack had been to Henry — too close, it was assumed, for comfort. Not a few of the other men who had been riding the circuit a little too steadily were, over that week end, unwontedly solicitous of their wives and gardens. But, the following week, when Henry, too, returned to the train, it was plain that the shaft which Mrs. Lister had aimed at her husband, had not only struck glancingly at his friend but had also sheared between the two. Their steps no longer joined naturally with each other's, when they greeted, it was with the creaking tact of constraint, and although they both were avoiding the Rainbow, they did not do so together.

When Henry, taking his month off early, took his wife down to Atlantic City, both the town and the smoker were relieved. It was felt that he had done the proper thing not only for his wife, but for the community. At present, for instance, it was neither natural to inquire after her, or to neglect to. But for a long time, even after things blew over, Henry would be a constriction on any company he kept — precisely because he had suffered no conventional loss.

Had he done so, however unusually, one could still have offered him the normal currency of condolence. One could have demonstrated one's fealty at the funeral parlor, or, meeting him at a later date, extended to him, according to the degrees of delicacy and acquaintance, either the mute clasp of the hand, or one of those basso-timbred remarks with which we acknowledge to one another that we are all as dust. Still later, after his sorrow was a little out of its black, one could have propelled him tenderly toward drink, as one propels a widow toward tears. As things were, however, Mrs. Lister, and death, in their brief affair together, had cuckolded Henry, had made of him, moreover, a man whose cuckoldry is known.

During the weeks of Henry's absence, Jack returned, little by little, to the Rainbow. Each evening he walked in earlier and stayed on later, until, rosy once more, he was back at the old routine. On those evenings when Denis judged him unfit to drive himself home the cabman was called. Or sometimes the cabby checked for himself, in a friendly sort of way.

On one of these evenings, just after Denis had made the call, Jack brought his glass down on the bar with a rap that raised Denis' startled glance from his paper, and leaned intently over the bar.

"Not the same around here, is it Denis?" he muttered. "Not the same." He looked into his glass, which he was swiveling in his hand. After a moment he looked up again. "It never will be the same," he said, in a voice suddenly free of rheum.

Denis, who, in his trade, witnessed few of the soaring denouements of drama, but often administered to its tag-ends and dispersals, kept his own counsel.

On another Monday night, this time late in June, Dicky, the judge, and Jack once more had the bar to themselves.

It was again the time of the judge's second round, and Dicky, again, had just breezed in. There was nothing oddly Aristotelian about this unity of time, space, and character; as must be clear by now, the very predictability of the Rainbow, the very reassurance of the way in which evenings spent there tend to blur into one long, continuous evening, is a part of its stock in trade. This night, however was the one on which Henry Lister chose to return.

When he walked through the door, which was screened now, and had been closed against the humming insect tide of summer, his manner in no way admitted that this was a return, or that there had been, at any time, a choice to be made. Denis, alone of the men there, was not surprised. On the faces of the other friends there was a momentary flash, like that on a mirror turned once against the light and laid flat.

To the right of Jack, who was farthest down the bar, there were three empty stools. Henry sat down on the middle one of these.

"Evening," said Henry. "Judge . . . Jack . . . Dicky . . . evening."

From the quiet chorus of greetings, Dicky's rose with verve. "Well look who's here! If he isn't a sight for sore eyes!" He walked over and pumped Henry's hand with unction. "Looking fit, boy," he added, in the low, secret tones of allegiance. "Real fit."

Behind him, the others stared into their drinks, but on Henry's face there was a singular look of gratitude. It was as if Dicky, in doing what might be expected of Dicky, had shown him that whatever else he had returned for was likely to be here too.

Now the other men began to talk, each punctuating his remarks with the helpful arc of his glass. They said little of local affairs, of all that can happen in a town, or a bar, while some one is away. They talked rather of things in the tenor of the times, of the National League and the American, of the price of government, and the probabilities of war. They spoke of the things people have to keep up to date on, no matter what has happened to them or where they have been.

Time passed, enough for the judge to leave and return for his final call. When the judge was on his last drink of the evening, Henry bought a drink for the crowd, sliding down a stool to the one next to Jack's. "How about you, judge?" he said. "Break down and have an extra?"

This was an old gambit, and the judge made his accustomed response. "Oh no," he said, frowning, made for the door, as if frightened, and left. Behind him, the men smiled at each other, taking pleasure in the foibles of their kind. On Henry's face there was again the look of gratitude.

After a while Dicky went into the alcove to play the pinball game. When the cabman poked his head with an inquiring look, Jack looked down at the floor. "Tell him never mind," said Henry's voice over his shoulder. "I'll drive you home."

It grew late, but the tawny light in the Rainbow deepened and mellowed, as if it, not the whisky, had the power to turn men rubicund or gray. The silence purred, that silence of the Rainbow which is like the purring of a great tom resting from the rat cries of reality, from the quest for cream, and the squeaky, flagellant voices of women. From time to time came the ratchety-slat of the pinball machine, than which there is no more aimless sound in the world. And after a while, it was the same.

In the Absence
of Angels

Before cockcrow tomorrow morning, I must remember everything I can about Hilda Kantrowitz. It is not at all strange that I should use the word "cockcrow," for, like most of the others here, I have only a literary knowledge of prisons. If someone among us were to take a poll — that lax, almost laughable device of a world now past — we would all come up with about the same stereotypes: Dickens' Newgate, no doubt, full of those dropsical grotesques of his, under which the sharp shape of liberty was almost lost; or, from the limp-leather books of our teens, "The Ballad of Reading Gaol," that period piece of a time when imprisonment could still be such a personal affair. I myself recall, from a grade-school reader of thirty years ago, a piece named "Piccola," called so after a flower that pushed its way up through a crevice in a stone courtyard and solaced the man immured there — a general, of God knows what political coloration.

Outside the window here, the only hedge is a long line

of hydrangeas, their swollen cones still the burnt, turned pink of autumn, still at the stage when the housewives used to pick them and stand them to dry on mantels, on pianos, to crisp and gather dust until they were pushed, crackling, into the garbage, in the first, diluted sun of spring.

We here, women all of us, are in what until recently was a fashionable private school, located, I am fairly certain, somewhere in Westchester County. There was no business about blindfolds from the guards on the trucks that brought us; rather, they let us sit and watch the flowing countryside, even comment upon it, looking at us with an indifference more chilling than if they had been on the alert, indicating as it did that a break from a particular truck into particular environs was of no import in a countryside that had become a cage. I recognized the Saw Mill River Parkway, its white marker lines a little the worse for lack of upkeep, but its banks still neat, since they came in November, after the grass had stopped growing. Occasionally — at a reservoir, for instance — signposts in their language had been added, and there were concentrations of other trucks like ours. They keep the trains for troops.

This room was the kindergarten; it has been cleared, and the painted walls show clean squares where pictures used to be, for they have not yet covered them with their special brand of posters, full of fists and flags. Opposite me is their terse, typed bulletin, at which I have been looking for a long time. Built into the floor just beneath it, there is a small aquarium of colored tile, with a spigot for the water in which goldfish must have been kept, and beyond is the door that leads to our "latrine" — a little corridor of miniature basins and pygmy toilets and hooks about three and a half feet from the floor. In this room, which has been lined with full-size cots and stripped of everything but a certain innocent odor of crayon and chalk, it is possible to avoid imagining the flick of short braids, the brief toddle of a skirt. It is not possible in the latrine.

They ring the school bell to mark off the hours for us; it has exactly the same naïve, releasing trill (probably operated electrically by some thumb in what was the principal's office) as the bell that used to cue the end of Latin period and the beginning of math in the city high school where Hilda Kantrowitz and I were among the freshmen, twenty-five years ago. Within that school, Hilda and I, I see now, were from the first slated to fall into two covertly opposed groups of girls.

On the application we had all filled out for entrance, there was a line that said "Father's Business." On it I had put the word "manufacturer," which was what my father always called himself — which, stretching it only a little, is what I suppose he was. He had a small, staid leather-goods business that occupied two floors of an untidy building far downtown. When my mother and I went there after a shopping tour, the workers upstairs on the factory floor, who had banded together to give me a silver cup at my birth, would lean their stained hands on barrels and tease me jocularly about my growth; the new young girls at the cutting tables would not stop the astonishingly rapid, reflex routine of their hands but would smile at me diffidently, with inquisitive, sidelong glances. Downstairs, on the office-and-sales floor, where there was a staff of about ten, one or the other of my uncles would try to take me on his lap, groaning loudly, or Harry Davidson, the thin, henpecked cousin-by-marriage who was the bookkeeper, would come out of the supply room, his paper cuffs scraping against a new, hard-covered ledger, which he would present to me with a mock show of furtiveness, for me to use for my poems, which were already a family joke.

The girls I went with, with whom I sat at lunch, or whom I rushed to meet after hours in the Greek soda parlor we favored, might too have been called, quite appositely, manufacturers' daughters, although not all of their fathers were in precisely that category. Helen's father was an insurance broker in an office as narrow as a knife blade, on a high floor of the most recent sky-scraper; Flora's father (of whom she was ashamed, in spite of his faultless clothes and handsome head, because he spoke bad English in his velvety Armenian voice) was a rug dealer; and Lotte's father, a German "banker," who did not seem to be connected with any bank, went off in his heavy Homburg to indefinite places downtown, where he "promoted," and made deals, coming home earlier than any of the others, in time for thick afternoon teas. What drew us together was a quality in our homes, all of which subscribed to exactly the same ideals of comfort.

We went home on the trolley or bus, Helen, Flora, Lotte, and I, to apartments or houses where the quality and taste of the bric-a-brac might vary but the linen closets were uniformly full, where the furniture covers sometimes went almost to the point of shabbiness but never beyond. Our mothers, often as not, were to be found in the kitchen, but though their hands kneaded dough, their knees rarely knew floors. Mostly, they were pleasantly favored women who had never worked before marriage, or tended to conceal it if they had, whose minds were not so much stupid as un-aroused — women at whom the menopause or the defection of growing children struck suddenly in the soft depths of their inarticulateness, leaving them distraught, melancholy, even deranged, to make the rounds of the doctors until age came blessedly, turning them leathery but safe. And on us, their intransigent daughters, who wished to be poets, actresses, dancers, doctors — anything but merely teachers or wives — they looked with antagonism, secret pride, or dubious assent, as the case might be, but all of them nursing the sly prescience that marriage would almost certainly do for us, before we had quite done for ourselves.

This, then, was the group with which I began; in a curious way, which I must make clear to myself, as one makes a will, it is the group with which, perhaps tomorrow, somewhere outside this fading, posthumous room, I choose to end. Not because, as we clustered, by turns giggling, indecisive, and impassioned, in our soda parlors, we bore already that sad consanguinity of those women who were to refuse to stay in their traditional places either as wives, whom we identified with our mothers, or as teachers, whom we identified with lemon-faced aunts, lonely gas rings, and sexual despair. Hindsight gives us a more terrifying resemblance. Not as women but as people. Neither rich nor poor, we were among the last people to be — either by birth or, later, by conviction — in the middle.

For the rich, even while they spun in their baroque

hysterias of possession, lived most intimately with the spectre of debacle. Like the poor, they were bred to the assumption that a man's thought does not go beyond his hunger, and, like them, their images of ruin were absolute. When the spectre of violent change arose in our century, as it had in every century, this time with two mouths, one of which said "Need is common!," the other of which answered "Therefore let thought be common!," it was the very rich and the very poor who subscribed first — the rich transfixed in their fear, the poor transfixed in their hope. Curious (and yet not so curious, I see now) that from us in the middle, swinging insecurely in our little median troughs of satisfaction, never too sure of what we were or what we believed, was to rise that saving, gradient doubt that has shepherded us together, in entrenchments, in ambush, and in rooms like these.

Two cots away from mine sits a small, black-haired woman of the type the French call mignonne; one would never associate her with the strangely scored, unmelodic music, yawping but compelling, for which she was known. She is here for an odd reason, but we are all here for odd reasons. She is here because she will not write melody, as they conceive melody. Or, to be honest — and there is no time left here for anything but honesty — as most of us here would conceive melody. But we here, who do not understand her music, understand her reasons.

Down at the far end of the room, there is a gray, shadowy spinster who knows little of heresies concerning the diatonic scale. She is here because she believes in the probity of mice. All day long now, she sits on her bed in a trance of fear, but the story is that when they came to the college laboratory where for forty years she had bred mice and conclusions, she stood at first with her arm behind her, her hand, in its white sleeve, shaking a little on the knob of the closed door. Then she backed up against the door to push it inward, to invite them in, their committee, with the statement she was to sign. Past all the cages she led them, stopping at each to explain the lineage of the generation inside, until, tired of the interminable recital, they waved the paper under her nose. Then she led them to the filing cabinets, unlocked the drawers, and persuaded them to pore over page after page of her crisscrossed references, meanwhile intoning the monotonous record of her historic rodent dead. Not until then, until the paper had appeared a third time, did she say to them, with the queer cogency of those whose virtue is not usually in talk, "No. Perhaps I will end by lying for you. But the mice will not."

She, the shadowy, weak-voiced woman, and I are alike in one thing, although I am not here after any action such as hers. They came quite conventionally to my suburban cottage, flung open the door, and loaded me on the truck without a word, as they had previously come to another poet, Volk, on his island off the coast of Maine, to Peterson, the novelist, in his neat brick box at the far end of Queens, to all the other writers who were alive because of being away from the city on the day it went down. Quite simply, they, too, have read Plato, and they know that the writer is dangerous to them because he cannot help celebrating the uncommonness of people. For, no matter what epithalamiums they may extort from us, sooner or later the individuality will reappear. In the very poems we might carpenter for them to march to, in the midst of the sanitized theses, the decontaminate novels, sooner or later we will infect their pages with the subversive singularity of men.

She — the biologist — and I are alike because we are the only ones here who do not cry at night. Not because we are heroic but because we have no more hostages for which to weep. Her mice are scattered, or already docilely breeding new dogma under the careful guidance of one of the trainees brought over here from their closed, incredible, pragmatic world — someone born after 1917, perhaps, who, reared among the bent probities of hungry men, will not trouble himself about the subornation of mice.

And I, who would give anything if my son were with me here, even to be suborned, as they do already with children, can afford to sit and dream of old integrities only because I, too, no longer have a hostage — not since the day when, using a missile whose rhythm they had learned from us, they cracked the city to the reactive dirt from which it had sprung — the day when the third-grade class from the grammar school of a suburban town went on a field trip to the natural-history museum.

Anyone born in a city like that one, as I was, is a street urchin to the end of his days, whether he grew behind its plate glass and granite or in its ancient, urinous slums. And that last year, when it was said they were coming, I visited my city often, walking in the violet light that seeped between the buildings of its unearthly dusk, watching the multiform refractions of the crowd, telling myself "I do not care to survive this." But on the way up here, when, as if by intention, they routed our trucks through streets of fused slag and quagmire (which their men, tapping with divining rods, had declared safe), I sat there in one of the line of trucks, looking dry-eyed at the dust of stone. Was it when the class was looking at the dinosaur, the *Archaeopteryx*, that the moment came? Was it while a voice, in soft, short syllables suited to his shortness, was telling him how a snake grew wings and became a bird, how a primate straightened its spine and became a man?

The room is quiet now, and dark, except for the moonlight that shows faintly outside on the hedge, faintly inside on the blurred harlequin tiles of the acquarium. Almost everyone is asleep here; even the person who rings the bell must be asleep, somewhere in one of the rooms in the wing they reserve for themselves. The little composer was one of the last who fell asleep; she cried for hours over the letter they brought her from her husband, also a musician, who wrote that he was working for them, that there could be glory in it, that if she would only recant and work with him, they would release his mother, and the daughter, and the son. The letter was couched in their orotund, professional phrases, phrases that in their mouths have given the great words like "freedom" and "unity" a sick, blood-sour sound. But tomorrow she will agree, and there is no one here who will blame her. Only the gray woman at the other end of the room and I sit hunched, awake, on our cots — taking the long view, who have no other. I sit here trying to remember everything I can about Hilda Kantrowitz, who was my age, my generation, but who, according to their paper on the wall, will not be here with us. Perhaps the last justification for people like me is to remember people like Hilda, even now, with justice.

What I see clearest about Hilda now is her wrists. I am looking back, with some trouble, at a girl who was never, except once, very important to me, and with some effort I can see thick braids of a dullish, unwashed blond, stray wisps from the top of them falling over her forehead, as if she had slept so and had not taken time for a combing. I cannot see her face from the side at all, but from the front her nostrils are long and drawn upward, making the tip of her nose seem too close to the flat mouth, which looks larger than it is because its lines are not definite but fade into the face. The eyes I cannot see at all as yet. She is standing for recitation, holding the Latin book, and her wrists are pain-fully sharp and clear, as if they were in the center of a lens. They are red — chapped, I suppose — and their flat bones protrude a long way from the middy cuffs. She does not know the recitation — she almost never does — but she does not titter or flush or look smart-alecky, the way the rest of us do when this happens. She just stands there, her eyelids blinking rapidly, her long nostrils moving, and says nothing, swaying a little, like a dog who is about to fall asleep. Then she sits down. Later on, I learn that it may be true — she may never get enough sleep.

We find this out by inference, Lotte and I, when the two of us are walking home together on a winter afternoon. That day, Lotte and I, who live near one another, have made a pact to spend our carfare on eatables and walk all the way home together. We have nearly reached 110th Street and Cathedral Parkway, having dribbled pennies in a store here, a store there, amiably debating each piece of candy, each sack of Indian nuts. In the west, as we walk toward it, there is a great well of dying light fading to apple-green over the river, which we cannot as yet see. The faces of the people hurrying past us have something flower-like and open about them as they bloom toward us and recede. We are tiring, feeling mournful and waif-like, with a delightful sadness that we breathe upon and foster, secure in the warm thought of home.

Down the block, there is a last, curving oasis of stores before the blank apartment houses begin. After that comes the long hill, with the church park and the hospital on the other side. Lotte has a last nickel. We walk slowly, peering into the stores. Next to a grill whose blind front is stencilled with lines of tangerine and false-blue light, there is one more store with a weak bulb shining. We press our faces against the glass of its door. It is a strange grocery store, if it is one, with no bakers' and bottlers' cardboard blurbs set in the window, no cherry brightness inside. Against its right-hand wall, galled wooden shelves hold a dark rummage of canned goods, with long, empty gaps between the brands. From a single line of cartons near the door on the lowest shelf, there is one hard, red glint of newness; these are packages of salt. Sprawled on the counter to the left, with her arms outflung between some box bottoms holding penny candy, there is a girl asleep. Her face, turned toward us, rests on a book whose thick, blunt shape we recognize almost as we do her. It is Hilda. Behind her, seen through the pane and the thin gruel of light, is the dim blotch of what looks like another room.

We confer, Lotte and I, in nudges, and finally Lotte pushes in ahead of me, her smothered giggle sounding above the rasp of a bell on the door. For a moment, it seems warmer inside — then not. A light is turned on in the back of the store, and we see that the second room is actually only a space that has been curtained off. The curtains are open. A woman comes forward and shakes Hilda angrily by the shoulder, with a flood of foreign words, then turns to us, speaking in a cringing voice. Candy? Crackers? How much money we got? Her face has a strong look to it, with good teeth and a mouth limned in blackish hair. In the half room behind her, on one of two day beds, a boy sits up, huddling in a man's thick sweater whose sleeves cover his hands. A smaller child clambers down from the other bed and runs to stand next to his mother. He is too young to have much hair, and the sight of his naked head, his meagre cotton shirt, and his wet diaper drooping between his legs makes me feel colder.

It becomes evident that Hilda and we know each other. I remember Hilda's cheekbones — sharp, and slowly red. The woman, all smiles now, moves toward us and lightly strokes Lotte's collar. That year, Lotte and I have made a fetish of dressing alike; we have on navy serge dresses with white collars pinned and identical silver bars.

"Little teachers!" the woman says. "Like little teachers!" She hovers over the counter a minute, then thrust a small box of crackers, the kind with marshmallow, into Lotte's hand. The baby sets up a cry and is pushed behind the woman's skirt. The boy on the bed stares at the box but says nothing. Confused, Lotte holds out her nickel. The woman hesitates, then shakes her head, refusing. Two fingers hover again over Lotte's collar but do not touch it. "Hilda will be teacher," the woman says. She makes a kind of genuflection of despair toward the place behind her, and we see that on a shelf there, in the midst of jumbled crockery and pans, is a man's picture, dark-bordered, in front of which a flame flickers, burning deep in a thick glass. She makes another gesture, as if she were pulling a cowl over her head, lets her hand fall against her skirt, and edges after us as we sidle toward the door. She bends over us. "Your mamas have what for me to sew, maybe? Or to clean?"

Hilda speaks, a short, guttural phrase in the language we do not understand. It is the only time she speaks. The woman steps back. Lotte still has the nickel in her open hand. Now Hilda is at the door. And now I see her mouth, the long lips pressed tight, turned down at the corners. She reaches out and takes Lotte's nickel. Then we are outside the door.

I do not remember anything about the rest of the walk home. But I remember that as I round the corner to my own street, alone, and am suddenly out of the wind, the air is like blue powder, and from the entrance to my house, as the doorman opens it and murmurs a greeting, the clean light scours the pavement. In the elevator, to my wind-smarting eyes the people look warmly blurry and gilded, and the elevator, rising perfectly, hums.

Lotte and I do not ever go back, of course, and we quickly forget the whole thing, for as the school year advances, the gap widens permanently between girls like us and those other unilluminated ones who are grinding seriously toward

becoming teachers, for many of whose families the possession of a teacher daughter will be one of the bootstraps by
which they will lift themselves to a feeling of security —
that trust in education which is the dominant security in a
country that prides itself on offering no other.

Then a bad time comes for me. My mother, after the birth
of another child, late in life, is very ill and is sent away —
to hunt for a warmer climate, it is said, although long afterward I know that it is a climate of the spirit for which she
hunts. Once or twice during that time, she is brought home,
able only to stand helplessly at the window, holding on to
me, the tears running down her face. Then she is taken
away again, for our windows are five flights up.

Business is bad, too, everywhere, and my father makes
longer and longer sales trips away from home. We have a
housekeeper, Mrs. Gallagher, who is really the baby's nurse,
since we cannot afford a cook and a nurse, too. She does not
wash my hair regularly or bother about my habits, and I
grow dirty and unkempt. She is always whining after me to
give up my favorite dresses to her own daughter, "a poor
widow's child in a convent," after which, applying to my
father for money, she buys me new dresses, probably with
the daughter in mind, and my clothes become oddly tight
and loud. Months later, after she is gone, it is found that she
has drunk up a good part of my father's hoarded wines, but
now no one knows this, and she is a good nurse, crooning,
starched and fierce, over the basket that holds the baby,
whom she possessively loves. Standing behind her, looking
at the basket, which she keeps cloudy with dotted swiss and
wreathed in rosy ribbon, I think to myself that the baby

nestled there looks like a pink heart. Perhaps I think secretly, too, that I am the displaced heart.

So I begin to steal. Not at home, but at school. There I am now one of the lowest scholars. I have altogether lost track in Latin, and when I am sent to the board in geometry, I stand there desperately in front of the mazy diagram, the chalk in my slack hand, watching the teacher's long neck, in which the red impatience rises until it looks like a crane's leg. "Next!" she says, finally, and I walk back to my seat. At test time, I try frantically to copy, but the smart, safe ones ignore my pleading signal. And once the visiting nurse sends me home because there are nits in my bushy, tangled hair. Thereafter, when I follow on the heels of the crowd to the soda parlor—my hand guarding several days' saved-up carfare, in the hope of finding someone to treat—the sorority is closed.

So, day after day, I treat myself. For by now, although there is plenty of food at home and Mrs. Gallagher packs me thick sandwiches (mostly of cheese, which she buys conveniently in a big slab to last the week) — by now I am really hungry only and constantly for sweets. I live on the thought of them, for the suspended moment when the nugget is warm in my mouth or crammed, waiting, in my hidden hand. And the sweets that comfort me most are those bought secretly and eaten alone. It never occurs to me to ask Mrs. Gallagher for spending money. At noontime, habitually now, I slip into the dark coatroom, where the girls' coats are hung, one on top of another, and, sliding a hand from pocket to pocket, one can pretend to be looking for one's own. And there, once again, I meet Hilda.

We meet face to face in the lumpy shadows of the coat-room, each of us with a hand in the pocket of a coat that is not her own. We know this on the instant, recognition clamoring between us, two animals who touch each other's scent in the prowling dark. I inch my hand out of the gritty pocket and let it fall at my side. I do not see what Hilda does with her hand. But in that moment before we move, in the furry dusk of that windowless room, I see what is in her eyes. I do not give it a name. But I am the first to leave.

Even now, I cannot give it a name. It eludes me, as do the names of those whom, for layered reason upon reason, we cannot bear to remember. I have remembered as best I can.

The rest belongs to that amalgam called growing up, during which, like everyone else, I learn to stumble along somehow between truth and compromise. Shortly after that day, I fall ill of jaundice, and I am ill for a long while. During that time, my mother returns home, restored — or perhaps my illness is in part her restorative. Her housewifely shock at what she finds blows through our home like a cleansing wind, and her tonic scolding, severe and rational as of old, is like the bromide that disperses horror. When I go back to school, after months of absence, I have the transient prestige of one who has been seriously ill, and with my rehabilitated appearance this is almost enough to reinstate me. Then an English teacher discovers my poems, and although I am never again a sound student in any other class, I attain a certain eminence in hers, and I rise, with each display coaxed out of me, rung by rung, until I am safe. Meanwhile, Hilda has dropped out of school. I never ask, but she is gone, and I do not see her there again.

Once, some ten years later, I think I see her. During the year after I am married, but not yet a mother, or yet a widow, a friend takes me to a meeting for the Spanish resistance, at which a well-known woman poet speaks. On the fringes of the departing crowd outside the shabby hall, young men and women are distributing pamphlets, shaking canisters for contributions. I catch sight of one of them, a girl in a brown leather jacket, with cropped blond hair, a smudge of lipstick that conceals the shape of the mouth, but a smudge of excitement on cheekbones that are the same. I strain to look at her, to decide, but the crowd is pressing, the night is rainy, and I lose sight of her before I am sure. But now I have reason to be sure. Yes, it was she.

It was she — and I have remembered as best I can. While I have sat here, the moonlight, falling white on the cast-down figure of the other waker, slumped now in sleep, showing up each brilliant, signal detail of the room in a last, proffered perspective, has flooded in and waned. I hear the first crepitations of morning. I am alone with my life, and with the long view.

They will tell us this morning that we must come down off our pin point into the arena. But a pin point can become an arena.

They will tell us that while we, in our easy compassion, have carried the hunger of others in our minds, they have carried it on their backs. And this is true. For this, even when they say it corruptly, is their strength — and our indefensible shame.

They will tell us that we have been able to cherish values

beyond hunger only because we have never known basic hunger ourselves — and this will be true also. But this is our paradox — and this is our stronghold, too.

They will tell us, finally, that there is no place for people like us, that the middle ground is for angels, not for men. But there is a place. For in the absence of angels and arbiters from a world of light, men and women must take their place.

Therefore, I am here, sitting opposite the white bulletin on the wall. For the last justification for people like us is to remember people like Hilda with justice. Therefore, in this room where there is no cockcrow except of conscience, I have remembered everything I can about Hilda Kantrowitz, who, this morning, is to be our prosecutor.

I will need to close my eyes when I have to enter the little latrine.

A Box of Ginger

FIVE stories below, the hot white pavements sent the air shimmering upward. From the false dusk of the awning, Kinny, leaning out to watch the iridescent black top of the funeral car, smelled the indeterminate summer smell of freshly ironed linen and dust. Below, he could see his father help the aunts into the car and stumble in after them, and the car roll away to join the others at the cemetery. The winter before, at the funeral of his father's other brother, everything had left from here, hearse and all. The house had been crowded with people who had entered without ringing and had seated themselves soundlessly in the parlor, greeting each other with a nod or a sidewise shake of the head, and for days there had been a straggling procession of long-faced callers, who had clasped hands with his father and mother and had been conducted, after a decent interval, to his grandmother's rooms, where she lived somewhat apart from the rest of the family. They had all come out clucking, "She's a wonderful woman, a won-der-ful old woman!," had been given coffee, and had gone away. Today, there was no one, and the wide glaring street was blank with light.

"Kinny, where are you?"

"I'm in the parlor."

"How many times have I told you to say 'living room'? Parlor!" His mother clicked her tongue as she came into the room. "Why didn't you go to the Park?" She walked toward him and looked at him squarely, something he had noticed grown people almost never seemed to have time to do.

"Listen, Kinny!" Her voice had the conspiratorial tone that made him uncomfortable. "You're not to let on to Grandma anything — anything about the funeral. It's a terrible thing to grow to a great age and see your children go before you." Her gaze had already shifted back to normal, slightly to the right of him and just above his head. "Don't lean so far out that window!" She turned and went into the kitchen to help Josie, the maid. His family never sat down to a dinner for just themselves; there were always the aunts, or the innumerable cousins, who came to pay their short devoirs to Grandma and stayed interminably at her daughter-in-law's table.

He wandered back into the room, dawdling. It *was* a parlor, very unlike the Frenchy living rooms of his friends. Opposite him, the wall was half covered by a tremendous needle-point picture, framed in thick, curdled gilt, of Moses striking the rock and bringing forth water at Meribah. "And Moses lifted up his hand," it said in the big Doré Bible, "and with his rod he smote the rock twice: and the water came out abundantly, and the congregation drank, and their beasts also." The faces of Moses and the Israelites were done in such tiny stitches that they looked painted, and there was a little dog lapping at the gush of water, which had minute, glistening beads worked into it. Diagonally across the room from the picture, the wreathed cherubim of a Vernis-Martin cabinet were flanked by a green marble column, on which poised an anonymous metal girl, arms outflung against a verdigrised apple tree, which sprouted electric-light bulbs.

He went over and fingered the Victrola, the only relatively new thing in the room. Slanting back on its lemon-oiled shelves lay all the newly acquired Red Seal records: Galli-Curci in the sextet from "Lucia"; the Flonzaley Quartet, whose sprigged mustachios he knew well from the Victor catalogue; and Alma Gluck, singing "From the la-and of the sky-ee blue" and then "wawtah" very quick. He would have liked to play that one, or "Cohen on the Telephone," but he was sure that he would not be allowed to today.

Walking into the hot, brassy clutter of the kitchen, he stopped at the icebox and drew himself a glass of water from a pipe than ran back into the ice chamber — a fixture in which his mother took pride but which he thought overrated.

"Can I have some of Dad's French Vichy?" He wasn't even sure that he liked its flat, mineral taste, but it was something of a feat to get it.

"No, you can't," said his mother, gingerly taking a tray of prune pockets out of the oven. "I can't be sending to the drugstore all the time. Catering to the fads and fancies of a lot of — A boarding house, that's what I'm running! You'd think they all *lived* here!"

"Mother, what did Uncle Aaron die of?" he said idly.

He already knew the answer. He rarely needed to ask an explicit question about family affairs. By picking up crumbs and overtones at the endless family gatherings, he had amassed his information. His Uncle Aaron had had pneumonia and had been convalescing on an upstate farm all spring. But his mother said, "Of old age, I guess," and gazed past him. Kinny's father, years older than she, was only a decade younger than the dead uncle. The family was getting down. His father had only sisters now. Kinny began to eat a prune pocket.

"You wait till you get to the table. One of these days, you'll burst!"

"Hattie!" a sharp, high voice called. "Hattie!" Then a small bell tinkled insistently.

"Go in and see what Grandma wants," his mother said. "Tell her the optician's man will be in this afternoon. And if she asks about a letter from Aaron, for goodness' sakes don't say anything!" She sighed. "I'm sure I don't know what they're going to tell her *this* time."

He idled slowly down the hall to his grandmother's bedroom, although he knew she had already been helped to her sitting room, where she spent most of the day. Light filtered through the half-drawn shades over the huge bed, with its wide panel of burled Circassian walnut, topped by a two-foot pediment of acanthus leaves. He swung himself onto the broad footboard, high as his shoulder. Up to it swelled the feather bed for which his mother was always

wanting to substitute a hair mattress. Everything was big
here — the looming wardrobe, where he had sometimes
hidden, choking, among the tight-packed camphored clothes;
the long chests, with their stretches of cold, fatty-looking
brown marble; the towering, grim-latched trunks.

On his confirmation day, just past, when one of the trunks
had been opened for the presentation of a gold watch with
a remote, scrolled face, he had been allowed to finger a
drawerful of Virginia Treasury notes with the serial numbers
marked by hand in brown ink, and a miniature envelope,
addressed in long-essed script — his grandmother's wedding
invitation, dated 1852. Still in her twenties, his grandmother
had married a man well past fifty, and her youngest son,
Kinny's father, had waited for marriage until he, too, was
almost fifty, so if you figured back, here was he, Kinny Elkin,
in 1924, with a grandfather, sunken in the ciphers of time,
who had been born in the eighteenth century. In his mind,
he saw the generations as single people walking a catwalk,
each with a hand clutching a long supporting rope that
passed from one to another but disappeared into mist at
either end.

"Kinny! Grandma wants you!" From the sitting room down
the hall he heard the familiar clank-clank of the gadrooned
brass handles on the sideboard. Grandma would be standing stiffly with the yellow box of preserved ginger, uglily
lettered in black, clutched in one knuckled hand, waiting
for the small afternoon ceremony that had been her only
apparent notice of him for as long as he could remember.
Reluctantly, he opened the door and went down the hall.

She stood there just as he had known she would, a dainty

death's head no taller than he, in the black silk uniform of age, one hand wavering on her cane, the other tight on the yellow box. The sparse hair, dressed so closely on the skull, enlarged the effect of the ears and the high nose with its long nostrils; the mouth, a mere boundary line for tributary wrinkles, firmed itself now and again. She was neat as old vellum, and though time had shrunk her to waxwork, it had left her free of the warts and hairs and pendulous dewlaps he saw on other old people. Her admitted age was ninety-three, but the family was of the opinion that she had concealed a few years, out of vanity.

"Here I am, Grandma." He moved toward her.

"Come here, child." Steadying her hand with his, she fumblingly placed in his palm a few tawny sugared slices of ginger. Under her waiting gaze, he placed a slice in his mouth and chewed. There was a small, acrid explosion in his throat; his eyes pinkened, but he swallowed obediently, knowing that she thought she was giving him a confection of which he was fond.

"Thank you, Grandma," he said thickly, his mouth on fire.

"All right, now." It was time for the other part of the ceremony. Slowly she leaned on his arm and he guided her steps across the room to the wicker armchair, into which she tottered, bearing down heavily on his shoulder and sending the cane in a rasping slide to the floor. Feeling in a pocket at one side of the chair, she brought up her glasses, polished the lenses with a bright-pink cloth, and put them on. Opening a folded afternoon paper, she began to read the headlines with the aid of a handled magnifying glass the size of a small saucer. The ritual was over. After supper,

Kinny's father would read her the articles she asked for, or, in his absence, Kinny would declaim them with careful dignity.

Dangling his legs from the dark old couch, he tried to place just what pulled at him so strongly in Grandma's rooms. Here in the sitting room, there were only a few steel engravings of Biblical scenes and a big, dark cloisonné pot stuffed with some brackish moss that never seemed to grow or die. Everything was still, but if he sat long enough, he felt the dim waves of history lapping at him, a moving, continuous stream that culminated in him.

He went restlessly toward the window and mooned out at the river. Maybe he could call for Bert, and they could go out and get some isinglass from the rocks that stuck out all over the ground across Riverside Drive. Bert maintained that if you could peel a whole clear sheet of it, it could be sold, like tinfoil.

"Call Hattie," said his grandmother fretfully. "Ask her if that optician man is coming." He had never heard her speak of the steady contraction of her sight, or of any other physical drawback, but Mr. Goldwasser came once a month and carefully did something — a plucking or trimming of the short, stiff eyelashes that tended to mat in the corners — which she thought beneficial.

"Mother said to tell you he's coming."

In the kitchen, his mother was discarding her apron.

"Here they come," she said. "Kinny, get away from that table." She brushed past him. Under Josie's reproachful, bovine stare, he took another prune pocket and stood at the head of the hall, watching.

Kinny's father, Aunt Flora and Aunt Amy, and his father's cousin Selena, old as the aunts, came in from the foyer. He thought that they looked furtive, as if they'd been doing something they shouldn't and were glad that it was over. Amy's face, wry and puckered now under her great bird's nest of iron-gray hair, was tiny and aquiline, with a short arc of mouth, and was supposed to be very like that of her mother as a young woman, but she had none of her mother's cameo neatness, and was always leaving untidy packages and having to come back for them, so that "something Amy left" had become a byword in the house.

"I think I dropped my gloves at the — " she said tremulously, and stopped. Nobody said the usual "Oh, A-amy!" His father groaned and walked heavily to the sideboard. Rooting in one of the compartments, he brought out the decanter.

"Now, Joe, do you think you'd better?" said his mother. "Come on, everybody. It'll do you good to eat something."

"Oh, leave him alone, Hattie," said Aunt Flora testily, jerking back the white pompadour that reared high over her rouged beak of face. Her inimical glance seemed to concentrate the momentary feeling of the others. Hattie hadn't just been through what they had.

Flora was the first to sit down at the table. Food, poker, and having the last word were her passions, in that order. "Come on, Amy, Selena," she said.

Usually, Selena wore puce or mustard or reseda green, but today she wore muddy brown, underlining the mud tints in her equine face.

Kinny's father sat at the head of the table kneading his

gray curls while the others ate, in silence. Kinny stole into
the kitchen and got out the bottle of Vichy. Tiptoeing into
the dining room, he placed the green bottle at his father's
elbow. He heard the doorbell ring and Josie ushering somebody into the parlor. She came to the dining-room door.

"Is here the eye doctor, Mrs. Elkin," she said.

"Take him on back to Grandma, Josie," said his mother.

His father stirred and groaned again. "What in God's
name am I going to tell Maw? I haven't the heart. I haven't
the heart, so soon after Nat."

"Never thought she should have been told about Nat,"
said Flora, brushing the crumbs from her black, bugled
front.

"What? Maw?" said Amy heatedly. "She seemed to catch
on almost as soon as it happened. She sits there half blind
and part deaf, and she hasn't been outdoors in ten years,
but try and fool her about anything in the family!"

Selena leaned forward with a faint flush. "You've been
fooling her about Aaron's letters, haven't you?" she asked.
"Hasn't Joe been writing them and mailing them ever since
Aaron went into a coma?" She looked around the table avidly.

"Aaron and I write — wrote — a lot alike," his father
said. "I just wanted to keep her from worrying at not seeing
him. I told her he might have to go out West." He turned
down his mouth wryly.

Selena leaned forward again, triumphantly. "Well, why
don't you just go on writing them?"

"It's a ghoulish thing to do." He rose and moved to the
window. Pulling up the awning, he wound the cord hard
around the hooked prong in the casement and stood looking

out. It was as if someone had suddenly thrown yards of blue soft stuff into all the corners of the room and veils had settled on the furniture. The white cloth gleamed. Across the wide avenue, the people in the building opposite had already turned on their yellow squares of light.

"She asked me four or five times yesterday," said his mother gently. "The last letter you had mailed from the farm is here, but I didn't know what to do."

The optician's man came to the door and peered at them obsequiously. "Er-hmm. I'm finished now." He held a little black bag in one hand and a round black bowler at his chest.

"Oh, yes, Mr. Goldwasser." His father turned from the window, reaching into his pocket for his wallet. "I'll see you to the door."

"Just a minute, Joe!" said Flora. She pushed back the dish in front of her and swivelled around in her chair. "Mr. Goldwasser."

"Yes?" He blinked at her politely.

"Can you tell us — how much can my mother see?"

"See?" he paused. "Why, she hasn't had an eye test in years, Mrs. Harris. It's hard to say. The lenses she has are the strongest made, and she's had them a good, long time." He shrugged. "She's lucky not to have a cataract, at her years. She sees enough to eat, does she not, and get around a little? What I do for her only makes her more comfortable, you know."

"Could she read, do you think?" Amy faltered, one of her bone hairpins sliding into her lap, where she worked at it nervously.

"Read!" He seemed surprised. "I can hardly think — maybe a block letter or two. You mean she still tries?" He shook his head admiringly. "A wonderful woman. Well!" He bowed and left them, followed by Kinny's father.

"They never will come right out with anything. Doctors!" Flora snapped.

"He's not a doctor, Flora," said Kinny's father wearily, returning to the room. He slumped into a chair. "I'm all worn out."

His mother was at the *secrétaire*. She held an envelope in her hand. "Better to get it over with, Joe, or she'll surely catch on. She complained about Amy and Flora not stopping in today."

Amy looked up vaguely and dabbed at her eyes with a napkin. "I just can't face her without showing something. I know I can't."

"Oh, Amy, be practical," said Flora. "How do you think we all feel? She's too old to suffer another shock like that. We'll have to warn everyone who comes in to see her. Go on, Joe."

"I'm no good at that sort of thing," he said, choking. "Not today, of all days."

"You've always been the one to read to her," said Kinny's mother. "She'd think it strange if any of us — "

Kinny found his voice, with a croak. "I — I read to her sometimes." He looked hastily around the table and then down at his shoes. Selena switched around in her chair and raised her brows at him.

"Why, Kinny!" said his mother in a slow, pleased way.

"I won't embroil the child in this!" said his father angrily.

"Little pitchers have big ears," said Selena with a caustic smile.

"I'm not a child." He hung his head and looked at his father sidewise. "She's used to me. I can do it." His voice trailed off weakly.

"After all, I was the one who had to go in and tell her about Nat," said his mother bitterly. "All of you avoid anything unpleasant."

"Maybe the child *could* do it," said Flora hurriedly.

His mother came around the table and thrust the envelope into his hand. "That's a good idea, Kinny. Just read to her, like you always do."

"All right. All right, all of you," muttered his father, not looking at him. "Just be careful, Kinny."

Now that their collective eyes, raw and ashamed, seemed to be pushing him out of the room, he felt uneasy. Carefully, he straightened the silver on his plate. There were several large crumbs on the floor next to his chair. With a prim show of industry, he picked them up, one by one, and put them on the cloth. Grinding his shoulder blades together, he left the room.

In the hall, he pressed his face against the cold, stippled wall. There were too many dark-angled halls in this apartment. He wished that the family would leave soon for the summer place, and thought with relief of the house, where you could dash straight through from back to front, out into the sunshine, slamming the door behind you. Stacked at a corner of the hall, rolled-up carpets wrapped in tar paper waited to be stored, giving out a drugged, attic smell. He flicked each one as he went by, rattling the paper in drum time.

Outside his grandmother's sitting-room door, there were several pictures that had been taken down and swathed in cheesecloth. He spent some time peering at these, trying to make out which was the one of the old bookshop and which the red-coated dragoon and his bride. Through the half-shut door he could see his grandmother in the unlit room. She was snoring softly, head back.

"Grandma," he said, his voice cutting the cobwebs. "It's me, Kinny." He went up and touched her lightly on the arm.

"Ah — oh. Yes?" The folded newspaper slid off her lap and she blinked up at him. Turning on the lamp beside the old cloisonné bowl, he laid the letter in her hand.

"A letter for you. Shall I read it?" It seemed to him that she hunched into herself like an old bird, listening.

"Where's your father? Where's Amy and Flora?"

"In the — in the dining room." He rocked back and forth on his ankle. "Can I use your paper cutter?"

She nodded, drawing her shawl around her, although the dank heat in the room made his lip bead. He got out the paper cutter, rubbing his thumb against the ivory hair of the girl on the handle, and slit the envelope. In the uninflected drone taught in the grade schools, he began to read his father's high, knotted script.

"My dear Mother: Trust this finds you well and in good spirits. Everything is fine here. The meals are good and the rooms are nice and clean. I miss seeing you and my dear family, but the doctor says that everything is going as well as can be expected, though he still would like to see me go out West this fall. Please God, we will all see each other before then. Keep well and do not worry if I write seldom, as there is very little news here. Your affectionate son, Aaron."

Rubbing the ball of one thumb ceaselessly in the palm of the other hand, his grandmother looked straight through him. He'd never noticed before how her head shook a little, as if blown by a slight, steady current from behind. "Read it again, Kinny," she whispered.

He read it again, more quickly, thinking that its phrases sounded a lot like the letters his father sent home from his travels — "please God" and "trust you are well," and signed always "Yrs. aff., Joe."

"Let me have the letter." Searching shakily in the side pocket of the chair, she brought out the thick, bevelled magnifying glass. Holding it almost under her nose, she inched it slowly along the letter, then the envelope, then back to the letter again. She sat for a long time with the letter in her lap; then a sharp movement of her arm sent the magnifying glass across the room, where it hit the couch and spun to the floor with the dull, rubbling sound of a top but did not break. He pressed his knees together, listening to the echo.

He saw that she was feeling for the cane. Frightened, he thrust it under her hand, but was reassured by the familiar heavy way she rested on him and pulled herself up in three marionette jerks. The two of them made their way to the sideboard. As she bent over the drawer, he saw the moisture from her eyes run six ways down the channels in her cheeks and fall into the drawer. Turning, she let her sticks of fingers brush his face in a dry gesture.

"Thank you," she whispered. "You were good to try." Thrusting the box into his hand, but not releasing it finally, she held her hands cupped around his, and for a moment, they rocked back and forth together, in a movement of complicity and love.

The Watchers

THROUGH the aqueous summer night, the shop lights along the avenue shone confusedly, like confetti raining through fog. From bench to bench in the narrow strip of park down the center, voices bumbled softly against one another, as from undersea diver to diver, through the fuzzy, dark medium of the evening.

Over toward the river, groups of girls and boys in their teens foraged for mischief and experience in the anonymous blur of the shadows, but Hester, bound to her mother, sat between her and her father's elderly cousins on a bench that they kept to themselves, repairing somewhat, by this separation, the *déclassé* gesture of sitting in the park. Across from them, in the big gray apartment house, Hester could see the long, lit string of their own windows — at one end the great, full swags of the Belgian-lace curtains of the living room, and around the corner the faint glow of her grandmother's night light.

Outwardly, it was because of her grandmother that their home swirled continuously with family company, but actually the visitors spent no more than a token time with the old lady, whom longevity had made remarkable but unapproachable other than as a household god. In reality, according to Hester's mother's exasperated comments, the visiting was a holdover from the bland, taken-for-granted gregariousness of the Southerner, whereby, in a rhythmic series of "droppings-in," in corner tête-à-têtes of intramural gossip, they all reaffirmed the identity of the family and of themselves.

Now, after the Sunday-night supper of cold cuts and cheese and pastry, most of the company had eddied away, and only three were left here with Hester and her mother — Rose and Martha, who lived in Newark and came only on Sunday, and Selena, who lived Hester did not quite know where but came most often of them all. Under the incomplete dark of the New York sky, their faces bobbled, uncertain and white, above their sombre, middle-aged dresses, and from time to time they pushed up sporadic remarks through the stifling heat.

"When does Joe get back?" asked Martha.

"Tomorrow morning," said Hester's mother. "This is his last trip for the year."

"Then you go to the country?" said Rose, with her plaintive whine, in which there was a hint of accusation.

"Yes, to White Plains. The same house as last year," said her mother, as if she regretted the disclosure. She would deplore their visits in conversation, behind their backs, but they would all come anyway, sending her into grudging paroxysms of hospitality.

"Not a breath stirring," said Martha, twitching her lip with a movement Hester could not really see but knew was there. Martha was a steady little person, dumpy-legged, with a face as creased and limited as her conversation. A milliner, working at home, she specialized in such oddly assembled trivia that Hester wondered often who bought them. She never went hatless and often appeared in rear-rangements of the same materials, so that the lilies of the valley of last week, detached now from their wreath of green leaves, turned up limp but enduring on the orange velvet toque of the week before. Martha's rooms, which Hester had once seen, had the same scattered look, as if her whole life were composed of bits of trimming and selvage that she endlessly, faithfully, turned and made do. On the speckled, polka-dotted, or mustily striped bosoms of her dresses, anchoring her together, there was always the gold brooch lettered "True Sisters," symbol of a Jewish ladies' organization that was her extracurricular glory. To Hester, it seemed that this must have some esoteric significance, about which she never dared inquire, since, in so doing, she would be delving impolitely into the personal springs that must lie under the trivia of Martha, would be asking of that cramped, undreaming little body, "Cousin Martha, to what is it you are True?" Another thing that lifted Martha from the ordinary was her tic, which consisted of a wetting of the lips and a side twitch of the mouth that occurred at regular intervals, whether or not she happened to be talk-ing. At first repelled by it, then fascinated by the way Martha and those around her ignored it, Hester had finally come to watch for it and dwell upon it, for it seemed to her a sign that obscure, eternal forces nudged even at the common-place Martha, twitching at her, saying, "Even under your polka-dotted bosom, under your bits and stuff, we are working, we are here."

Next to Martha, Rose, her younger sister, whom she intermittently supported, made the muted small sounds that were meant to indicate delicately that her digestion, as usual, was not acting well. Rose was the only one of her father's cousins whom Hester disliked. With the slack shoulders and drooping neck of the invalid, she sloped inward upon herself, as if it were only by an intense concentration on her viscera that their processes might be maintained, as if the fractional huff-huff of her heart would go on only so long as she was there to listen and bid it. About her there was always the cottony, medicinal smell of indefinite ailments which would never be confirmed, Hester felt unsympathetically, except by that astringent confirmer, death.

"Want some soda, Rose?" asked her mother. "We could run across to the drugstore."

"No. I'll be all right," said Rose, satisfied that her distress had been noted. She turned toward Hester, whose stolidity she was always trying to court. "Getting such a big girl!" she said. "Why isn't she at camp, with Kinny?"

"She has to make up her algebra at summer school," said her mother. "Besides, she says fourteen and a half is too old for camp."

"Fourteen years. Imagine!" said Martha, the involuntary spasm flicking over her face, like an oblique comment. "Why I can remember her in her bassinet!"

"Yes," said Hester, in a dreamy urgency to say it before anyone else could. "How time flies!"

"Hester!" said her mother.

From Selena, sitting rigid, unyielding, in the supple currents of the dark, came a stifled snort, whether of amusement or disapproval Hester could not quite tell. Of all the adjuncts to their household, Selena was the most constant and the most silent. Spare and dark-haired, the color of a dried fig, she wore odd off colors, like puce and mustard and reseda green. Although they did not become her, she carried them like an invidious commentary on the drab patterns around her, and her concave chest was heavily looped with the coral residue of some years' stay in Capri as an art student, in her youth. She was the secretive spinster remnant of a branch of the family that had once been rich, so her concealment of her circumstances and her frequent presence at meals provoked occasional discussion as to whether she was still rich but miserly or had lost her money. "Poor Selena," Hester's father had once commented. "She's hungry for *people*." With her face pursed in her habitual contempt for the family of Philistines, she sat at their table nevertheless, partaking voraciously of something more than food.

"Where does Selena live?" Hester had once asked her mother.

"Oh, somewhere in Brooklyn," her mother had answered indifferently. "In the house her mother left her, I think."

"Were you ever there?"

"No-o." Her mother had shaken her head, amused, with the depreciative smile of those for whom Manhattan was New York. "Someone once told your father she'd sold it. No one really knows, though. She keeps very close."

"Did you ever see any of her paintings?"

"She painted me once, holding you, just after you were born. Mother and child." Her mother had laughed slightly.

"What was it like? Can I see it?"

"Oh!" Her mother had thrown up her hands, then brought them together, shaking her head in derision. "I don't know where it went. I suppose she took it back."

It had been Selena's mother, the old grandmother's elder sister, who had sent the grandmother, long ago, from California, the silver service with the pistol-handled knives the family still used at dinner parties. With it had come the large cup and saucer, covered with beaten gold, that Hester and her brother, long used to hearing their father say, "That cup's over a hundred years old!," had taken to calling "the hundred-year cup." Translating this to Selena, Hester privately visualized her as living in the narrow, high rooms of one of the single houses she associated with the very rich — in a house, perhaps, that was a kind of hundred-year cup of treasure, from which the humdrum touch of people would be inscrutably barred.

Leaning forward, Hester almost touched her hand softly to the coral hanging like strips of rosy twigs on Selena's flatness.

"I like it better this way," she said, "than round and smooth, like my baby beads."

"Oh?" said Selena, raising the furry circumflexes of her eyebrows. "And why do you like it better?"

Accustomed to asking why, rather than to being asked, Hester hesitated, startled. "It's more real," she said, finally.

"Real?" echoed Selena, the harsh tang of her voice thrusting the word forward, like a marble, to be felt and examined.

Through the dimness, Hester could see her long, saffron face poised on one side, listening, weighing the word and Hester's use of it.

Emboldened by attention, Hester went further. "Where did you get them all — the corals, I mean?" she asked.

"On the island of Capri." There was a sostenuto, heroic pride in her tone, in the lifting of her chin, that stirred the others, Hester thought, to embarrassment and impatience.

"We'd better be going in," said her mother. "It's getting damp."

"What's it like — Capri?" asked Hester, imitating Selena's drawn-out Italian vowel.

"You might see for yourself someday," said Selena.

"Me?" said Hester. "Why, nobody ever travels in our family, except Daddy."

"No?" said Selena. She leaned back on the bench, turning her face away from them, shaking the loops on her chest slightly with her bony fingers, producing the slack sound of imperfect castanets.

"I really think . . ." said Hester's mother.

Across the street, through the sluggish air, there floundered a white, heavy figure, moving in starts and stops. It was Josie, the maid. As she ran, she gesticulated sidewise with her arms, wailing, "Meesis Elkin! Oh, Meesis Elkin!," so that the people on the other benches turned to look at them.

"Oh, that girl!" muttered her mother.

Josie had reached them. "Granma!" panted Josie. "I took in the eggnog and I could not vake her. I think — Come quick!"

"My God!" said Hester's mother. "Joe will never forgive me!"

Like a chorus, the three other women wheeled protectively around her, and, gathering up their long skirts, they all ran stumbling across the street to the entranceway of the apartment house. Catching up as they were entering the elevator, Hester tugged at her mother's elbow.

"Forgive you for what?" she said.

"For letting his mother die while he's away," said her mother, staring ahead. As they entered the apartment, she turned savagely on Hester. "You go in your room and *stay there!*"

The house filled almost magically with people, so no one noticed that Hester remained in the dining room, taking it all in, sitting alone on one of the ring of chairs that were ranged around the table like supernumeraries in a play. First had come the doctor, routed from his Sunday-night card game, on whom her mother and Rose and Martha hung, as if on a priest, as he came out of her grandmother's bedroom now, solemnly nodding his head. Selena followed, a step behind them.

"Selena, phone the others, will you?" said her mother.

"Be glad to," said Selena gruffly.

What perplexed Hester was that she really seemed to be glad to. Sitting straight as an upholstered stick in front of the phone, she handled it with import, calling Flora and Amy — the daughters of the dead one — and all the lesser relatives who would be offended if they were not among the first to be notified. Using the same formula as she got each number, she said not "your mother" or "your grandmother," as the case might be, but "Aunt Bertha." "I'm sorry to tell you," she would say, "but just a little while ago Aunt Bertha . . ."

It was the closest to death Hester had ever been. Seated there alone at the great, round communal plate of the dining table, she felt herself all over, inwardly, for the abrasions that were proper to the circumstance, but found none — nothing except a shameful sense of excitement over an extraordinary drama in which everyone unwontedly exposed himself. Aunt Flora, who had come, in answer to Selena's call, from her apartment a block away, had superseded Selena at the phone, as befitted a daughter of the deceased. With tears ruining the rouge on her aged-soubrette face, under the high white hair, she called number after number, bearing up remarkably until she got her party and identified herself, at which point she quavered, "Oh, Nettie!," "Oh, Walter!," and then burst into what seemed to be welcomed, cathartic tears.

I never cry over anything except myself, thought Hester guiltily, wondering whether, if they noticed her, they would expect her to be crying. Worriedly, she tried to think of something that would make her cry, but nothing stirred in her except the neutral, dispassionate awareness, the ignoble spur of interest.

Dispossessed from her post, Selena came and sat down opposite her. She raised her brows in surprise at Hester's still being up but said nothing, and her cheeks were hennaed with an unaccustomed tinge of participation. For a long time, the two of them sat there watching, while between them grew a tenuous thread of communion, as between two who sit at the edge of a party or a dance, sipping the moderate liqueur of observation, while around them swirl the tipsier ones, involved in a drunkenness the watchers do not share.

At last, Hester's mother, who had been busying herself like a distraught hostess, noticed her and, with an enraged whisper, sent her away to bed. Since Hester had always felt that her mother in the presence of others talked to her rather for their benefit than for hers, the scolding rolled off her numbed, sleepy head, and she walked away untouched, undisturbed, down the long hall to her room, past the closed door of her grandmother's bedroom. As she stood tentatively in the darkness of her own doorway, the door of the bedroom opened, and two men came out carrying a long wicker hamper, which they set down, securing the creaking cover, and then swung between them again, with a servile, devotional gait.

Sleepily pulling off her clothes, she was almost too tired to go through her nightly custom. She climbed onto the radiator under the window and stood there splayed out against the pane, feeling the familiar welling triumph of being suspended in space above people. She thought emulously of Selena, who remained apart, uninvolved, in her rich security of far places experienced, of distances apprehended. Bending down, she completed her ritual, sniffing at the jointure of the window, at its dark smell — a mixture of moisture and dust and the sharpening cool of night.

In bed, the last thing Hester remembered was the word "capri," which rolled toward her, in her mind uncapitalized, like a small coral bead, but when the brilliant afternoon sun woke her the following day, and sent her nuzzling down into the bedclothes, with their comfortable odor of orris and of her carelessly washed flesh, it was the hamper she remembered. She saw again the sickening rhythm in which the two men had moved — conspirators, shuffling out between them the surprisingly dowdy appurtenance of death.

She reached under the bed, and, drawing out one of the books she kept secreted there, held it in her hand for a long time, but when her mother opened the door and surveyed her exasperatedly, she still had not opened it.

"I never saw a more indifferent girl!" said her mother. "Your father's home and carrying on terribly. Everything falls on me!" She walked around the room, flipping back the bedclothes, picking up objects with the grim, abstracted compulsion of the housewife, the straightener, the manager. "Get up!" she said fiercely. "The funeral's at four o'clock. Make yourself a little decent, for once. Get that hair out of your eyes!"

"Am I going to the funeral?" asked Hester.

"No," said her mother. "Your father doesn't approve of children being exposed to death." Then she walked to the window and, slowly, measuredly, as if she were moving in time with a conventional elegy prescribed for the occasion, pulled the shade down firmly all the way to the sill and left the room. Chilled, Hester watched her go, wondering, as she dressed herself haphazardly, if the hard little correctnesses — the properness that seemed so difficult to acquire — crept in gradually as one grew, or whether, on some unspecified name day, one came of age, stepped into the finished, hypocritical shell, and was suddenly grown.

Once outside her door, she found the rest of the apartment sequestered and dim, as if some orderly person had just left, after solicitously muting the colors, numbing the sounds, strewing over everything the careful bleach of bereavement. From behind the closed door of her grandmother's sitting room, she heard a low rustle of voices and, centered in them, an indescribable retching sound.

She ran toward the warm neutrality of the kitchen. Josie was flusteredly scrabbling at batches of cookery, for which she had rooted out almost everything from the vast storecloset.

"Don't touch nothing!" Josie said hastily. Then, contrarily, she pushed toward Hester a plateful of *palacsinta* — thin pancakes stuffed with sweetened cottage cheese or melted jelly, which she would never make on command but which would appear suddenly when she had been moved, perhaps, by homesickness for her own country or by a sense of occasion. As Hester ate, Josie hovered over her, sighing.

"T-t-t!" said Josie, rocking back and forth. "Is too bad." Again Hester felt the flicker of guilt, as if someone had twanged a string inside her and had found it slack, without resonance.

She left the kitchen and crossed the hall to the dining room. Peering into the parlor through the French doors, dully masked with net, she made out a corner where chairs had been drawn aside to make room for what must be the coffin. Parting the doors stealthily, she went in, planning to see for herself the thing to which children must not be exposed.

As she entered, a figure seated in front of the coffin moved slightly. Terror of the unimaginable jumped in her, for the figure was tiny, bent, and dressed in spare black, as her grandmother had always been. Expelling her breath, she saw that this was a stranger, whose china teeth and thick, glossy brown wig, rimming her face like a hat, were both too big for her, giving her the appearance of a Punch-and-Judy doll that had been excessively repaired.

Hester drew back, but the woman, misinterpreting her withdrawal, motioned toward her ingratiatingly, with a custodian's pride. Drawing Hester compellingly to the coffin's side, the woman then stood with her hands bunched together at her neckbones, her bright, avian stare cocked sidewise as Hester looked down into the box.

Less wrinkled, whiter than in life, Hester's grandmother extended her short length in the box, with the same finished, miniature look she had always had, with the same natural dignity. At any moment, Hester felt, she might unlock her eyes and say, "But how could you think I would not handle *this* decently, properly, too?" Shrinking from the gross casualness of the woman attitudinized beside her, Hester wavered nearer the box, and when she turned and ran from the room, it was from the live woman that she ran.

In the hallway, she collided with the hatted figure of her mother, and for a moment that soft collision with dim, powdery fragrance, with the half-remembered enveloping warmth of babyhood, clouded the barrier of properness between them.

"Who's that little old woman in there?" Hester whispered.

"Who? Oh, she's a professional watcher," said her mother. She was carefully draping a thick veil over her hat. "Your grandmother was Orthodox, you know," she added with a certain disdain. "Someone has to be with the dead until the burial, the next day."

"Is that her *job?*" Hester whispered.

"It's a volunteer society, I believe. I suppose women who have no other . . . I suppose one gives them *something*," her mother said impatiently, with a final shake of herself. "Go stay with Josie," she added, frowning.

Lingering in the hall, Hester watched her mother listen at the sitting-room door for a minute and then knock.

"Joe," said her mother, "it's almost time."

The door opened and Hester's father came out, surrounded by the hovering women: Flora and Amy — his sisters — and the cousins Rose and Martha. Selena was not among them. Her father looked blindly ahead of him, and half groans, the replica of the awful sound she had heard before, still shook him.

"Joe," said her mother, "get ahold of yourself!"

He raised his head. "Ahold of myself!" he said. He bent his head again, and the women closed around him — the red-eyed, solicitous sisters first, then the border of cousins — and, moving their dark caravan slowly, steadily, they passed through the dim foyer and out the apartment door.

Hester tiptoed to the empty kitchen. Through the half-open door of Josie's room, she saw her sleeping on her bed, openmouthed. Shutting the back door of the apartment softly behind her, Hester ran down the five flights of service stairs into the back court of the apartment house. Making a wide circle, she arrived at the front entrance and unobtrusively joined the audience of children and passersby that flanked it.

All along the street, the line of black cars waited in heavy perfection, closed to the great blond sea of the sun. From both corners, people converged upon them, like a stream of ants, and were met at the center by a gentleman with a fixed look of gravity, who murmured something to each of them, referred to a list in his hand, and, nodding, conducted them to one or another of the cars.

Next to Hester, a woman nudged another. "The family," she mouthed.

Now the grave man's look deepened, became even more carved, as, with a stooping, comma-like posture, the list disregarded, he handed Hester's parents and the aunts into the central car, bearing them along almost on his arm, as if they were the veritable royalty of grief. Behind them, Martha, in an aspiring headdress poised like an aigrette on a sparrow, and Rose, straighter than usual, were shunted into one of the rear cars by an assistant. By now, the cars were full, and the stragglers who still came were people, unfamiliar to Hester, who did not seem to expect to go with the cortege but passed on, whispering among themselves, into the building. Four men, dressed the same, and of a size, like dummies, emerged, carrying the coffin. At the curb they paused, shifting the weight between them, then slid it neatly into the hearse.

The carved gentleman raised his hand officiously toward his assistant. "All set," he said.

Suddenly, walking alone, came Selena. Even today, she had been unable to resign herself to black and wore a dress the rubbed blue of plumskin, whose texture seemed flattened here and there by years of waiting in a box. Without the insignia of her coral, she looked somehow bereft, but she walked toward the gentleman in austere pride, on her cheeks the henna tinge of the night before.

The gentleman looked discomforted. "Only the immediate family," he said placatingly.

"I am a member of the family," said Selena in a secure contralto, but one hand opened and closed at her chest, seeking the reassurance of the corals, as if she might at any moment add, "The member from Capri."

Bending nearer, the gentleman murmured an inquiry and agitatedly checked her answer against his list. "I am sorry," he said in buttered tones, "but there seems to have been an oversight. Do you wish me to check with a member of . . ." He paused and allowed a delicate insinuation of disapproval to affect his face.

"No," said Selena in a rusty voice. "Never mind."

He bowed. "The family," he said consolingly, "will receive friends of the deceased upstairs when they return." He flicked a nod to his assistant, and with a sinuous deftness they inserted themselves into the hearse, which pulsed into a motion that reverberated sluggishly down the line of cars.

In a few minutes, the street was almost empty of cars and onlookers, except for Hester, who had crept behind one of the ironwork grilles in the courtyard, and Selena, who remained as if held by a need to see the last of the cars inexorably gone. Standing there in the open light of summer, she looked to Hester at once bizarre and dusty, like one of those oddly colored bits of bric-a-brac that seem mysterious and compelling in the back of the store but, when brought to the light by the excited purchaser, are seen to be lurid and unsuccessful. When the last car had gone, Selena stood there for a moment, her hand still nervously groping on her chest; then, slowly, with a ragged, indecisive gait, she turned and walked away.

Hester saw her recede down the long block, until she vanished around the corner. In her mind, like a frieze, she saw the added-up picture of Selena, always watching tentatively, thirstily, on the fringe of other people's happenings, and fear grew in her as she became suddenly aware of her own figure, standing now in the hot sun. It was watching, too.

The Sound of Waiting

Sᴜɴᴅᴀʏ was the day you hung around listening to the echoes of yourself. In the fat silences after dinner, everyone hovered, holding on to the dwindling thread of yesterday's routine, wretchedly waiting to join it to that of tomorrow. Outside, the soft tearing sound of the traffic rushed people to innumerable delights and conclusions; inside the ticking room anticipation swelled like a bell that was never sounded. Laved, in fresh clothes, the body thudded, poised for its adventure, until the sharp definitive click of the lamps slid the day down from the hope of change into the pigeonhole of reality.

For all, for everyone except his father. For him, Sunday was a kind of justification, whose rest he took in the biblical sense, a patriarch relaxing superbly from converse into the sleep where he lay now, the mock-fierce mustache stirred by the breath from the hidden kindly mouth, the delicately made spatted ankles, out of another era, crossed sideways on the sofa.

If he moved now, his father would stir irritably, muttering "Eh? Where're you going now? Can't you spend a day with your family?" for, to his almost tribal sense of family, outside interests were always to be secondary, and — with the dwindling of his own family contemporaries by death — the attainment of adulthood in his children and their increasing focus outside the home seemed to induce in him a pathetic rage, almost as if over a breach of allegiance.

If wholly awakened now, he would rise to potter testily with his cigar, roughing the newspapers back into coherence with mutterings against the disorderliness of the rest of the family, or, if fate provided an attentive Sunday visitor, settling benignly again into the anecdotes that eructated like bubbles from the ferment of his memory. "Salesman's talk," his mother called it, for to her his father's expansiveness, always a continual social embarrassment to her aloofness, had become even more of a reminder that his father was really an old man now, that the long gap of age between them would never again be bridged. His father was old enough to be his grandfather — had the gap between his father and himself never really been bridged at all because of this alone, he wondered? Or was it because his father belonged to the last outpost of a generation which regarded its children as the final insignia of a full life, perhaps, but always as extensions of its own identity, interposing between them and it a wall of glass, through which the pattern of daily intimacies might be filtered, but through which the self-contained globe of a child's private world was forever inadmissible?

Over and above the flood of real "goods" that his father sold twinklingly, unfailingly, in the backslapping cama-

raderie of business, his father *was* a salesman, he thought
— a salesman of the past. Rootless though the family had
long been, in the shifting way of the apartment dweller, because of his father they had continued to live as if they still
had attics and cellars, their closets and rooms crammed with
the droppings of generations, the yellowed inanimates that
had pitilessly survived the transient fingerprints of the flesh.
When he, his son, had looked about him at the mass of
young men at college with him, he had felt that, compared
to his own, their backgrounds were as truncated, as flat,
as their tidy one-step-above hire-purchase homes, where a
family picture was an anachronism that must not mar the
current scheme, where the old and worn must immediately
be slip-covered with the new. And it had seemed to him
then, that although he had never had the permanence of a
homestead, of the landed people, he was rooted, he had
been nourished, in the rich compost of his father's reminiscence.

But now, in the taut room, where the silence stretched
like a wire vibrating with impulses that were never heard,
he felt suddenly that his father had always been as remote
to him as a figure in a pageant, or as a storyteller between
whose knees he had been gripped, enthralled, but whose
recitative backward glance had never bent itself to him.
And torn, half by a jealousy for that panoramic experience,
that sweep of life that he and his own contemporaries might
never duplicate, he looked across at his father with regret,
feeling that he, the son, had listened indeed, but had never
himself been heard. From all the crooning corners of his
childhood he could hear his father's teasing, crowing voice:

"Sure, boy. I've been everywhere! I've been to Europe, I-rup, O-rup, and Stir-rup!"

As in the faded primary tints of a lithograph on a thumbed calendar, he could see, he could almost *remember* the dusty provincial streets and lanes of the post-Civil War Richmond of sixty-five years ago, and the little boy with black Fauntleroy curls being dragged along by the gaunt, arrogant Negro woman, past the jeers of the street urchins.

"Plenty of professional Southerners talk about their colored mammies — but Awnt Nell — she was a real woman. Freed woman too, but she would never leave your grandmother. And proud of my curls — as if they were her own boy's! Kept me getting in fights over 'em. Then she took to follering around behind me, 'til I went to Maw and cried to have 'em cut off. Stayed with us too; wouldn't go away even after Paw's business went bad with the rest." . . . The remembered voice went on, like a record he could pluck out from the years at will.

"Guess I should have been a lawyer. Always wanted to be." Yes, his father would have liked that — the poised strut in front of the attentive jury, the poured-out display of the enormous, sometimes inaccurately pronounced vocabulary.

"Left school too early. Heh! The Academy — that's where we went in those days — all religions alike. Academy of St. Joseph. That old harridan there — Miss Atwell — she never did like me. One day she said to me 'Joe! Come up here!' And she had the ruler in her hand. Now your grandmother — she never raised her hand to the eight of us, and she kept us all in line. I wasn't gawn to stand for any ruler rapped on

my knuckles. So I walked up there . . . and I stood there
. . . and I put out my hand. And when she raised the ruler
I took it, and broke it over my knee, and threw it out the
window. I left there and I never went back. Never. Only
time I ever made my mother cry. Swore I would never make
her cry again. I was a good son, and I didn't. But I never
went back there again."

Then the first job — the grocery store — almost like the
stereotype beginnings of the self-made American, but with
the imprint of the fastidious Joe, the *bon vivant*, the *fin de
siècle* beau-to-be, already implicit in the tale.

"That herring barrel! Seemed 's if everybody who came
into that store wanted herring. So I'd reach my hand down
in that cold slithery mess of stuff and haul up one of those
herring. Ugh! Quit that job as quick as I could . . . went
into a lawyer's office licking stamps. At the end of a week
I went to Mr. Morris (your grandmother was married from
his house) and I said 'Mr. Morris, I want to leave.'

" 'Why Joe,' he says, 'what's the matter?'

" 'Mr. Morris,' I said, 'my tongue is sore!'

"He sat back and laughed and laughed. 'Why Joe,' he says,
'we'll give you a sponge!' "

In the stereopticon of his mind he could see his father's
hand reaching down into the barrel, but somehow it was
not the raw hand of the thirteen-year-old boy, but the elegant knotted hand with the raised blue veins and the brown
diamond finger ring, in the graphically illustrative gesture
he had seen again and again, the hand he saw now drooping over the sofa, lifted imperceptibly now and again in
the current of slumber.

Glancing back into the dimness of the foyer, he could see the huge triple-doored bookcase, its sagging shelves stuffed three-deep with the books that had been his father's education. He thought of his own studies, the slow acquisition of the accepted opinions on the world's literature, sedulously gathered from the squeezings of the compartmented minds of his professors, the easy access to the ponderous libraries with their mountains of ticketed references as available as his daily dinner. Yet it had been years before he could mention a book of which his father had not heard. "Baldassare Castiglione!" his father would say, taking the book from his hand, rolling the syllables on his tongue. *"The Courtier!* My God, it must be nearly fifty years since I saw that!" For a moment a formless eagerness has trembled on his own lips, as if he might say at last "What do you — ? — This is what I — Let us exchange . . .'" but the book would be handed back, the sighing revelation had not been made, the moment passed.

All during the early years while his father had been selling soap for a Quaker merchant in Philadelphia he had also been studying Italian in the evenings so that he could read Dante in the original, or picking his way through Horace and Ovid with the aid of the "trots" that would have been forbidden to him had he gone to college. On one shelf of the bookcase, *Mademoiselle de Maupin,* the *Mémoires de Ninon de Lenclos,* and a row of Balzac stood as evidence of the years in New Orleans, where, only in his twenties, but already the dashing representative of "Motley and Co., Manufacturers and Perfumers, Founded 1817," he had, according to his own testimony, spent half his time at Antoine's, and the rest on the pouting bosoms of Creole ladies of good family. On the other shelves *Rasselas, Prince of Abyssinia,* a red-edged set of Thackeray, and some funereally bound Waverley novels were jumbled together; copies of Burns, Mrs. Browning, and the *Heptameron of Marguerite of Navarre* might be interlarded with the Victoriana of Quiller-Couch, Sir Edmund Gosse, and an old copy of Will Carleton's *Farm Legends.* In the brown dusk of the foyer they all melted together, holding under their dusty gilt a repository of his own childhood, for on them he had fed also, and from them had been drawn the innumerable orotund tags of his father's conversation.

Stealthily he rose and went to the window. On one of the nearby tables lay the broken-backed copy of Pope from which his father often quoted, its cover scrolled and illuminated to look like a church window. Published by William P. Nimmo of Edinburgh. He had never realized until he was almost grown that his father's vaunting chant was not literally true; that his father had never actually been out of America. Where had he picked this up? He opened it and read the inscription: "J. Henri Elkin, Mar. 26th, 1882," and beneath that, underlined with flourishes, "sans puer et sans reproche." With a smile for the insouciant motto and the error in spelling, both so typical of his father, he grimaced at his own forgotten inscription underneath, written in the brash pencil of his sophomore year: — "J. H. Elkin, Jr., Jan. 5th, 1929. De gustibus non est disputandum."

"Europe, I-rup, O-rup, and Stir-rup," he thought bitterly. He had believed it of his father; in a way it was his trouble that he still believed, not only for his father, but for himself. The phrase had meant for him all the perilous seas beyond the casement, all the width of the future that lay before the "compleat," the "whole" man, all the roads to Rome. When he heard the foghorns lowing on the river, the phrase sometimes came to him still, with a quickening of inexplicable delight and unease.

Now suddenly its echoes brought to him, with an association he did not understand, the image, sharp and disturbing, of the glass of anise on Anna Guryan's table.

Shutting the image out, he turned his back to the sleeping figure and stared out the window, past the blurred palette of the park with its motley strollers, to the strong blue of the river, which struck through the tentative spring air like a flail against his sight. It was not too late to fill the day that was draining away from him with one of those commonplace devices for seeking human warmth, a dinner, a date, a movie — the little second-rate enterprises where there was always the chance, after all, that reality might explode upon one in the exchange of a word, a recognition, an embrace.

He turned over a roster of people in his mind: the earnest young men of his own age, whose conversation would turn inevitably from books and jobs to girls, with the fascinated allusiveness of inexperience, or the gauche young girls tricked out in the bright dresses, shrill patter, and the finger-snapping gestures of allurement that would lead them not too improperly to their goal of a doctor or a dentist.

There was no one, nothing that he could scrape up that would serve as a palliative for the driving sense of alienation, of constriction, that sent him out more and more on his free Saturday afternoons and Sundays, prowling the dim drowsy art galleries, standing before each picture as if it were a window to a world, yet always subtly conscious of the current of people moving behind him, their dress and their speech, and of how he, in his stance before the picture, looked to them. Or he would walk the brilliant mid-town streets briskly, as if he had a destination, savoring the expensive color and movement, glancing at the great carved upheaval of buildings with a pride almost of ownership, until a dusk the color of melancholy blended all the outlines of faces and buildings in a brooding preamble to the great play of light that was to come.

Then he would flee into the haven of some small restaurant, always somehow, the wrong one, where, under the slack gaze of the waiter, he would choose from the menu with an exaggerated sense of the importance of his choice, and eat his dinner slowly, head bent, whetting himself against the knife of his solitude, until home seemed at last the only destination there was, and he would rise and go. Home, exhausted, ready at last for its commonplaces, he would let himself into the dim clogged air of the hall. Nodding over a book, his father would look up to mutter his half-irritated "Where've you been?" and to all the sounds and stimuli singing in his head the remark would be like a shutter, closing down between the halves of himself, and he would reply guiltily, almost as if he had been lying, "*Just around*" . . . or "*Nowhere.*"

Tomorrow, delivered once more from the disturbed, uninhabited spaces of the week end, he would sink almost gratefully into the round of his job, that job which was so far from the context of his home that he could never have expected it to be understood at home, had he ever been asked. Along with the hundreds of others spewed out by the colleges the previous summer, into professions that had no room for them, he had found a place in the only employment where there was room, in the vast framework of the city's welfare department. He had been at it almost a year now, toiling up the steps of tenements in neighborhoods he had never before seen, delivering his blue and yellow tickets to existence to his one hundred and forty families.

In the beginning it had been exciting, almost romantic, to penetrate deeper into the unknown capillaries of the city that he loved, finding, in the midst of the decaying East Side tenements, the rococo hoardings on an old theatre that had been the glory of his father's day, seeing a date on the crumbling pink façade of the stables on Cherry Street where the peddlers kept their nags, reading the layered history of the city like a palimpsest. But lately it had seemed more and more as if he were immured in the catacombs of a daily round, from which he would never work himself up into the clear.

He thought of the families he would be visiting tomorrow, each of them like a little aperture into the world that really was. There would be the whine of Mrs. Barnes, born, raised, and married, on some form of aid, but with the steamy smell of comfort somehow always in her kitchen. "Now there's William," she would whisper, with her sidelong glance. "Poor boy, he's a diabetic, you know. He needs special food." And the boy William would stand there with his over-sharp, delicate Irish face averted, his hunched shoulders straining away from notice. In the next house, Mr. McCue, "brassworker for thirty years," would once more exhume the badge to which he clung, the bank book showing the $4000 savings which had lasted three and a half years until now, and on his broad brick face there would be the usual look of puzzlement at what could happen to a man who had worked and done what was right and proper.

This was Yorkville, but over on 95th, near the river, the stunted inhabitants had seemed to him at first like a race of anthropophagi whose faces he never would be able to distinguish one from the other. Stumbling once through one of these buildings, in search of a family that was about to be evicted, he had passed through room after room in which the varicolored women, sprawling on daybeds, or huddled around tables in shrieking atonal conversation, had paid no more attention to him than if he had been invisible. Passing on into the dark center of the building, he had found himself in a black windowless room where there was no light but the red sparks flying out from under the frying pan in which a girl with wild Hottentot hair was cooking fish. She had looked at him indifferently, as though she would not have been surprised if he had grown from the floor, and had replied hoarsely to his question: "Family? There ain' no *families* here." He had stood there for a moment in the disoriented blackness, feeling himself shrunk to a pinpoint, a clot in time, and it had seemed to him that he had penetrated to the nadir of the world, where personality was at an end.

In the quiet planes of the room behind him, his father's

breathing went on, like a gentle, insistent susurrus from a world that had been. Only that morning, the radio, playing Grofé's "Grand Canyon Suite," with its swaying theme of the donkeys, had reminded him, as always, of one of his father's favorite anecdotes, one that, as a boy, he had never heard without an ache of emulation, of desire for the avenues of action that would one day be his.

"That summer I was eighteen, Mr. Motley sent me out all the way to San Francisco. Some responsibility for a boy, but I'd been working there in New York for him for two years, and he trusted me. Travelling on the Union Pacific, met a man in the dining-car, Colonel Yates, big mine-owner out there. Took a liking to me and invited me to stop off the next day and go down to one of his mines. I thought I shouldn't stop off to do it, but he said 'Listen, boy! *You want to see the world, or not?*' So the next morning I got off with him, but when he saw me he said 'God, boy! You can't go down a mine in those clothes!' You see, those days, every salesman of any account dressed to look the part, and I had on a three-button cutaway and a top hat.

"'Colonel,' I said, 'these are the only clothes I have.' And it was true, too. He shook his head, but we went on anyhow, and when I saw that canyon we were going down into I wished I'd stayed home in New York. A drop down into nothing for miles, and the only way to go down it was a narrow little trail not wide enough for a man. What they did, they used these little Kentucky single-footers, mincing from side to side, one foot in front of the other. Well, I looked at that donkey, and he looked at me, and I flipped up my coat-tails and got on. Went all the way down that canyon with my top hat on my head, and my coat-tails hanging down behind!"

The picture of his father, middle-sized, dapper, in the raw West of the eighties, brought back momentarily the pride and tenderness which had always been a part of the feeling that he supposed was meant by the term "filial." As a boy he had never minded that his aging father had never joined in the baseball games like other fathers, or taken him swimming, for in his tales of the trotting-races at Saratoga, the fights in which John L. Sullivan had battered round after round bare-knuckled, the cockfights held secretly in a grimy cul-de-sac in New Orleans, had been the heady sense of an apprenticeship to the masculine world. And blending always with that gamy recall of the sporting world of the nineties had been the undercurrent that was implicit in his father's knowing allusion, in the slow spreading smile of reminiscence, in the anecdote lopped off at an unsuitable part — an undercurrent that spread beneath his talk, moving provocatively under the lace of words like a musky perfume — the sense of beautiful women.

Outside he could almost feel the subtle pressing of the sooty spring air, snubbing against the pane like an invitation. In his mind he traversed again the grim woodcut streets of his "district" wondering whether Sunday brought easement there, or whether there too, it was like a vacuum sucking the inhabitants into a realization of despair. He thought again of Anna Guryan, whom he had first visited two days before.

The address had been that of an old tenement off Hester Street, most of the occupants of which were already on his list. On the paper-strewn gritty stoop he had met old Mr.

Askenasi, evidently on his way to the barber-shop for the pre-Sabbath "shave with hot towels" to which the Jewish men, young and old, clung, throughout the humiliation of being on relief, as to a last shred of independence and manhood, though there might be no cholla for the table, or little tea for the glass.

"Guryan?" The old man had shaken his head. Then he had drawn back, pressing his lips together. "Taht one? You mean she will get on the relief too?" Throwing up his hands, he had exploded in a torrent of Yiddish. Then he had drawn closer. "Listen!" he had whispered in English, patting the other rhythmically on the shoulder for emphasis. "Since she has been here that door has never been closed. All hours of the night, men going up there. It is a shame for the other people in the house. Listen . . ." But at the other's guardedly professional lack of response he had broken off and gone on down the stoop, turning once to shake his head angrily with a glance that was like an accusation.

He had found the door easily enough, on the ground floor to the left, as one entered the dank focus of smells that was the hall. Most of these apartments led directly into the kitchen from the hall, and his first impression as he entered was that the kitchen was far cleaner than most, partly perhaps because the furniture was so sparse and there was no litter of food, or evidence of where it might be stored. He had been prepared for one of the volubly evasive women who were flocking to the protective disguise of the relief rolls, or who were occasionally referred to him by the probation officers on a promise to "go straight," many of them fat and aging, distinguished from the neighborhood women only by their carefully hammered hair and the clear aseptic finish of their make-up.

He had found her sitting at the table, a small, deceptively young woman, her figure thin and unexuberant under the dark blue dress. To his first surprised glance she had appeared dated somehow, possibly because of the way she wore her hair, close to her head in the casque effect of the flapper period, with its sharp black wings pointed flatly against the white-powdered oval of her face. As she answered his formal questions in the slurred, unclassifiable monotone of her speech, her poised hands folded in her lap, he had been reminded of that Egyptian cat in the Museum, which had come through the erosive sands of the centuries and the trembling hands of archaeologists, to sit finally on its chill pedestal in the echoing gallery, regarding the modern world still with its glance of impenetrable dislike. He had found himself avoiding her unreflecting onyx gaze, which slid over him as if she were making some secret assessment of himself. Ruffled, he made a show of scrawling her answers in his notebook, a technique he hated and almost never used, partly because he had always felt too keenly the humiliation of those who were being probed, and partly because he had found soon enough that the intonations of misery were not easily forgotten.

She had just been discharged from the hospital, she said. and had told them she had no means of support. They had told her to go to the relief. The janitor of the building was a friend of hers and had let her have the apartment free until the end of the month, since the rent collector had already made his rounds. The furniture? The janitor had lent her an old bed for the back room, and the kitchen set had been left by the previous occupant.

In this neighborhood, where everything was sold and exchanged down to the very nail-parings of existence, where old men sat in front of stalls formed by their knees and the sidewalk, haggling over used shoestrings, a few screws and bent nails, even a single boot, he had known this could not be true. Even so, the kitchen table stood between them, irrefutably new, its white baked enamel surface shining like a statement.

Raising his head to confront her with this, he had found that he could not say the bald words, and across the table he had seen a thin film of triumph slide over the opaque slits of her eyes. With a gesture of finality she had risen for the first time and pulled the chain on the light bulb that hung over them. Behind her the two blotches of windows sprang forward onto his sight like two frames holding forth the dark. On one uncurtained sill there was a bottle. Reaching for it, she drew a shot-glass from the table drawer, and poured.

"Anise. You have some."

He had refused, out of a conflict of reasons that were obscure to him, the least of which was that the rules of his job would have forbidden it. Gathering up his pencil and notebook, he retreated to the door, explaining hurriedly that he would let her know the decision of the office.

She had opened the door for him, clasping it close against her to let him by.

"All right. You come back and let me know. Any time." A smile had widened her lips, spreading like oil, and just before the door closed, looking down, he had seen, like a revelation, an intimacy, the pink inner orifice of her mouth.

Hurrying into the half-tones of the evening, all the way home in the swaying push of the subway, even now, as he leaned against the pane, he had retained in his mind, like the central core of an undifferentiated whirl of feeling, the image of the glass of anise waiting on the table, light radiating from its icy viscous white as from a prism.

Behind him on the sofa his father still slept, punctuating with his breath the quiet that pressed on the eardrums like a weight. For one warm moment it seemed almost possible to him that, shaking the slumped shoulders, touching the brown crepe hand, he might awaken his father beyond the present minute, into an awareness of him at last; in some long shared conversation, that backward elegiac glance would for once be forced fully, openly, on him, and he might say, "Father . . . was it so for you? . . . For what is it I wait?" Instantly the fantasy shrank, and he winced at the picture of the clumsy byplay that would really occur, knowing that between them lay the benumbing sleep of the years, a drowse from which it was not possible to awake.

Outside the window there was sound, motion, involvement, even if only in one of his long aimless hegiras through the streets. He turned slowly and left the room. Down the long hall, the first door open on the right was that of his parents' bedroom. Entering, he picked up the hairbrush from his father's chifferobe and began brushing his hair.

Even here, the sense of his father's youth was present to him, like a minimizing mirror in which he saw himself. On the high chifferobe, neatly arranged, as were all his father's accouterments, lay the silver toilette set of which the hair-brush, with a handle, in the old style, like a woman's, was a part. There was a broad clothesbrush, then a narrower hat-brush, and a small stud-box, all with heavy intricately wrought tops of silver repoussé, in the center of each the flat shield with the monogram JHE, and a soap-box, like a huge Easter egg of plain silver, on its top the embossed head of a nymph with twining silver hair. One saw odd pieces of simi-lar sets now, unwanted and forlorn, in the dusty jackdaw windows of Third Avenue junk shops, crowded among the sad statuary and implements of a period that was done but had not quite yet slipped into the cherishable patina of the antique. Holding the brush, he remembered.

"Who do you suppose is in New York?" his father had chuckled from behind the *Times* one morning at breakfast, sitting there easy and fresh, wearing one of the dandified light silk ties and curious scarf-pins from the collection that crowded his dresser drawers, a mode that his wife could never persuade him to discard, that was as much a part of his style as the faint odor of cologne left clinging to the crumpled towels in the bathroom.

"Letty Danvers," said his father. "Arrived on the *Queen Mary*. Stopping at the Great Northern. That's where they all used to stop in the old days."

"Who's Letty Danvers?" he had asked, savoring the grace-ful English name on his tongue, sensing already, in his mother's stiffness, the possibility of mischief. In the portfolio of family pictures there were several of unidentified women, mostly in profile, in the clear unshaded photographic style of another day, staring large-eyed and proud from under the curled fringe of their bangs. His mother would never confess to a knowledge of who they were. "Ask your father!" she would say, tossing back her head.

"Why she was what they'd call a 'diseuse' now, I guess," said his father reflectively. "The greatest of her day. I knew her, my God — years ago. You know that silver dresser set of mine? She gave me that."

"I always thought Mother gave it to you." His mother shook her head, tightening her lips.

"Maybe I'll go and see her," said his father. "Talk over old times."

"Kind of an elaborate present, wasn't it?" he had said, watching his mother.

"Not for those days," said his father musingly, from behind the paper. Then, looking up, he had met his son's arch glance, his wife's bridling look.

"Purely platonic!" he had growled. "Purely platonic, I assure you!"

"Hmmm," said his mother.

His father had slammed the paper down on the table. "My God, Hattie, it was forty-five years ago. She was years older than I was. Why she must be damn near eighty years old!" He had stamped away from the table in a self-conscious huff, mock-angry, but pleased. For once, vanity had wrung from him the nearest allusion to his exact age that he would ever make. . . .

Like a boy building over and over the same tower from blocks grooved with use, he could reconstruct the times of his father. He watched him living with his young French friend, Louis Housselle, in the Prince Albert Apartments, home of the fancy theatre set of the day and their ardent hangers-on. He saw him, a few tables behind Diamond Jim Brady, betting on that famous marathon of the appetite, or leaning intimately toward women over the small round tables, almost eclipsed by the velvet swoop of their hats. In yachting clothes he leaned back jauntily, legs crossed, the hand with the ring draped easily on the chair; posing for a portrait he held the aquiline medallion of his profile sideways, the black curls cropped almost to the bone, on his shapely upper lip a feather of mustache. . . .

The rough bossing of the brush handle had left a pattern on his clenched hand. With a conscious, almost defiant gesture, he set the brush down askew in the long neat silver line. Stepping softly down the back hall, he let himself out of the apartment door. Avoiding the elevator, he hurried down the five flights of stairs and out into the street.

As always before, the milling streets gave him back the feeling of action; the air blowing against his face set up an unreasoning tingle of anticipation. Flower shops, pastry shops, and stationery stores were all open; people wove in and out of them on their beelike errands. Down the perspective of the side street he could see the olive-green buses, their open decks crammed with people in vivid spring hats, rocketing by like floats.

He ran down the intervening blocks. Wedging himself onto one of the buses he followed the line of people up the swaying stair. Upstairs the deck held the rows of people like a well-arranged tray, everyone coupled and spruce as a crowd just out of church, varied only by the restless dots of children.

They rolled by the Museum and stopped. Clutching the change in his pocket, he thought of getting off there, but while he wavered between indecision and habit, the bus heaved on. He knew the Museum too well, anyhow, particularly the American Wing, where he had wandered too many desultory afternoons, past the snub, diffused faces of the Cassatts, the small violent Homers, pausing longer at the moon-racked Ryders, held for minutes before the unfathomable Sargent "Madame X." By now it was too well-defined a theme in his routine of hope and ennui.

At Fifty-seventh Street he got off and walked east. Stopping at the Kraushaar Galleries, he peered in at the blank dark doors. Several weeks ago they had been open one afternoon and he had wandered in. No one had intercepted him, and he had found himself in the midst of an "opening show" of French paintings, mostly Renoirs. Behind him the silky authoritative murmurs of approval or contempt went on almost unheard, for he had been held in front of the Renoirs by a shock of familiarity, of recognition. They sat there, the women of his father's day, stiffly at their garden tables, under their enormous hats, in spade-shaped bodices, their faces and hair fretted by light and leaf shadow; in the dim blur of their boudoirs they curved over dressing tables their bodies of impermeable lavender and rose.

Today the window held a few Flemish *genre* paintings in overpowering frames, and the interior was lifeless and dark. The plate glass gave him back a dusky astigmatic version of himself. He turned away. No one was coming down the long suave street; held there, gripped again by the drag of time draining away, he felt that no one would ever come. He waited, avoiding the knowledge of where he wanted to go. Time passes, he thought; perhaps one should go toward it. Far down the street, the thin line of the horizon was like a sealed eyelid waiting for him to lift it, to expose the huge wink of the future.

Turning on his heel, he walked slowly eastward down the long street, which grew more squalid with every step, with the inevitability of a declining curve on a graph. At Second Avenue he mounted the rickety stairs of the "El" and caught a train that was just winding its parabola into the station.

Jigging past the tenements in the settling dusk he watched the window scenes as they flicked by: a woman leaning over a sink, a man stretched out with his feet up, somnolent in a chair. Since childhood he had done this, hanging out from the tops of the buses on Fifth to catch a flash of a paneled drawing-room, a great brown wall of books, or people, muffled and vague behind a shimmering curtain; riding past in the veiled evening he had fondled these glimpses and enlarged upon them.

In this neighborhood he could now, because of his work, fill out the scenes to the last detail of mohair armchairs and cracked, calendered walls. He knew well the sameness of the life that went on behind those window lights that were so sterile and graceless from inside — the endless arias of family quarrels, and the blind grapplings of love. Even so, as he walked or rode along, each appearing lamp stood out like a lighthouse of warmth that drew him in his lonely role of beholder; each was an evocation of possibility.

At home now, their own lamps would be turned on soon for supper, and his father would rise, yawning, to go to the table, happy and complete in his belated role of paterfamilias if the family were all present, grumbling and swearing one of his strange oaths that were like no one else's, if one of them were missing. *"Phantasmagoria!"* he would shout. "Where in God's name does that boy find to go?" In the landscape of his mind he watched the image of his father collapse and dwindle with distance, heard the sonorous echo of his voice trickle and die; in his mind he pursued the image and the echo for a last minute, before he let them go.

At the last station, he got out. It was still a long way to Hester Street, and he walked the odd-angled asymmetric streets with a delaying step, remembering his first experience of them last year, when the heat of summer had been a great blunting hand pushing the people out of doors, the whole area had had the smell of a dying fruit, and his clothes had felt like a cage.

He stopped at last in front of the house. It must have rained recently down here. The carts and hagglers had deserted the block, leaving in the gutters pools that gave back the last light of the sky. A slate-colored breeze from the river blew brinily against the empty, peeling doorway.

He walked inside and put his hand on the doorknob. Over on the river the foghorns spoke, making over and over their slow mysterious statement. He had never been able to decipher it until now. It is the sound of waiting, he thought. *The sound of waiting.*

Cupped in his hand, the oily doorknob spread under his palm as if he were touching a slowly widening smile. He knocked. He heard a light-chain being pulled on in the back room, and the high-heeled sound of footsteps coming toward the door. After the first compromise, he thought, all others follow.

Looking back through the open doorway, he saw the dome of the day melting downward irretrievably into the river. One by one, in the great pitted comb of the city, the evocative lights went on.

The Pool of Narcissus

When the Muschenheim limousine slid up to the curb, like a great, rolling onyx, it had hardly stopped before the chauffeur, in broadcloth cerements, leaped out and flourished open the door. Mrs. Muschenheim emerged slowly, her enormous bulk divided and encircled with ruchings, the elegiac balloon of velvet that compressed her black pompadour looking like the knob on the chess queen.

Hester, watching intently from a cramped stone niche in the courtyard entrance, where she had been sitting in Sunday-afternoon stiffness, knew that this arrival was the signal that the birthday party at the Reuters' was about to begin. While Mrs. Muschenheim stared before her with majesty, the chauffeur reverently brought forth several cake-boxes of a whiteness and size that drew awed murmurs from the kids around the entrance, then bore them smartly behind his employer as she lumbered through the courtyard and into the apartment house on her way up to the Reuters', on the ninth floor.

Hester could never decide which attracted her more — the elaborate sweets or the solemn pageantry of the Reuter family life. Sometimes she was given tastes from the boxes of mocha torte or glazed cherries when Clara, the fifteen-year-old granddaughter of the Reuters, descending to Hester's twelve-year level on bored, boyless afternoons, asked her upstairs, and the two of them hovered hopefully on the periphery of the stately orgies of pastry, coffee, and talk.

The Reuters belonged to the solid phalanx of upper-middle-class German burgher families that moved in its own orbit in New York. During the first World War, just past, the women had learned to knit by the jerky American method and had bought Liberty Bonds stolidly, but through this period, as always, they lingered over the coffeepot on smoky winter afternoons, did their hair leaning over rivulets of scalloped dresser scarves made by the daughters of the house, and married off their sons and daughters to one another — not by compulsion but through the graceful pressure of cocoa parties together at the age of ten and dinner parties at the age of twenty.

Hester detached herself painfully from her cold seat, permitted herself one superb glance around at the other kids, who did not share her entrée, and followed Mrs. Muschenheim in, just slowly enough not to catch the same elevator. She went up to her own family's apartment, four floors below the Reuters', and scurried back to her room, sliding off her coat. Because of the inactivity of Sunday afternoon, her new dress was still fresh. Ramming her barrette to a firmer hold on her hair, she burrowed in her bureau drawer for the tissue-wrapped handkerchief that would serve as her ticket of admittance to the birthday party. Holding it by its rosette of ribbon, she slipped out of the apartment, climbed the four flights to the Reuters' floor, and rang the bell. Clara opened the door.

"Oh, h'lo, Hester," said Clara, her eyes on the little package.

"'S for your mother's birthday," Hester muttered, and thrust the package at her.

"Oh, *thank* you, Hester! She'll be pleased," said Clara with sweet artificiality. Both were aware that a handkerchief was not to be considered a real present but, rather, a kind of party currency. Then Clara dropped her adult tone. "Listen! Guess what!" she said, and hurried Hester along the hall toward her mother's bedroom. Going past the piles of tissue paper and ribbon on the waxed foyer table, turning her head to peer back through the living-room doorway at the people gathered inside, Hester thought there was no place for a party like the Reuters', where all the material panoply of life was treated with such devotion.

Both Mrs. Reuter, the grandmother, and her sister, Mrs. Enke, rivalled Mrs. Muschenheim in size. Their mammoth hips swelled like hoop skirts under their made-to-order dresses. Behind her nose glasses, Mrs. Reuter's enlarged blue eyes melted innocently in the genial arrangement of red pincushions that was her face. From Mrs. Enke's more elegant profile, wan folds draped away sculpturally, as befitted her long-standing widowhood. In this citadel of women, which included Clara and her mother, Mrs. Braggiotti, Mr. Reuter might have felt oppressed had he not been equally large, and likely to find, on his four-o'clock return from the lace business, various Adolphs and Karls, of severe clothes and superb, gold-linked linen, who had already deserted the garlanded cake plates for a bottle of schnapps, over which they would discuss the market. Once, Hester had even seen the German consul there, his domed head rolling and stretching out on his creased neck like a sea lion accepting the deference of the crowd. When, on such occasions, Mrs. Reuter's eyes turned too explicitly to Hester's grubby play dress and battered knees, the two girls played in Clara's room with the frilled doll that had belonged to Clara's mother, or made exploratory tours of the other bedrooms.

All the bedrooms were of such complete neatness that Hester had never been able to imagine the Reuter women as really going to bed at all, but saw them moving serenely through the night ready to meet the first caller of the day, their hair unawry, their watches pinned to their waists. To her, these rooms full of starched bolsters, where every plane was animated with linen and crisped with laces, seemed the ideal toward which any girl would aim her hope chest, but sanctuaries, nevertheless, in which it was improbable that any of the natural functions went on. The closet floors were not cluttered with stray shoes or saved boxes, and in the dresser drawers there were no broken earrings tumbled among cards from the upholsterer, bits of cornice off the mirror, and odd ends of elastic. Each object, useful and needed, reposed in a wash of space and calm. Mrs. Braggiotti's room had, in addition, the aura of the romantically pretty woman.

In this room, Hester and Clara always went to the dresser first, passing from the etched-crystal tray, with its kaleidoscopic row of perfume bottles, whose number and style

varied with Mrs. Braggiotti's admirers, to the rosy pincushions, where, among hat daggers and florists' pins, sometimes
lay two great dinner rings, with rows of huge diamonds in
pavements of smaller ones. These, Clara said, had been the
Reuters' gift to her mother on her marriage. Who or what
Mr. Braggiotti was or had been, Hester had never been told.
If she conceived of him at all, it was as an alien, a kind of
slim, Italianate poniard that had once got embedded mis-
takenly in the firm dough of the Reuter household.

What drew Hester most in this room was the shoes. Clara
would ostentatiously swing open the closet door, and there,
in the soft cretonne pockets that covered it from base to
top, were her mother's thirty pairs of small, high-arched
shoes, some in leathers of special kinds — snake or piped
kidskin — but most of them dyed in pale costume shades
that resembled in their gradations of color the row of sewing silks on a drygoods counter. Looking at them, Hester
could see Mrs. Braggiotti, who, with her tilted nose, masses
of true-blond hair, and bud mouth, was what every shag-
haired girl staring into the Narcissus pools of adolescence
hoped to see. Hester thought of her as she had often met
her, riding down serenely in the elevator, a pale, wide hat
just matching the flowers in her chiffon dress, a long puff
of fur held carelessly against the faintly florid hips. Mixed
with this image was a more perplexing vision, of Mrs. Braggiotti at the piano, where she played Chopin with much
ripple and style but wearing a pince-nez that mercilessly
puckered the flesh between her brows, giving her the appearance of a doll that had been asked to cope with human
problems. Hester preferred to think of her as endlessly float-

ing from one assignation to another in an endless palette of costumes that matched.

It was toward Mrs. Braggiotti's dresser, then, that Clara pulled Hester, pointing out the huge bottle that stood on the tray, eclipsing all the others. "George gave it to her, just now!" said Clara.

"Who's he?"

"He's *in love* with her."

It was only recently that Hester had learned not to giggle at the term. Now the phrase fell on her ear like something dropping softly, momentously, from a tree.

"Is *she* in love with *him?*"

"How should I know?" Clara stared down her nose at her. Apparently, Hester had again made one of the major errors that were always emphasizing the age gap between them. Obviously, to Clara's way of thinking (which must also be the adult one), the important thing was to *be* loved and to enjoy all the gestures thereof.

Without stopping to inspect the rest of the room, the girls went back along the hall and edged into the overheated living room. Mrs. Reuter was with a group near the door, and on the far side Mrs. Braggiotti, this time without the pince-nez, was playing the piano for a number of gentlemen gathered around her. "How pretty your dress is, my dear! Did your mother make it?" panted Mrs. Reuter, her glance approving Hester's cleanliness, one hand blotting the drops of sweat from her hot face and just preventing them from falling on her gray satin prow.

"She did the flowers." Hester looked down doubtfully at the lavender voile, its color harsh against her olive-brown hands. All over its skirt and sleeves, unsuccessfully tiered to hide her lankness, large bunches of multicolored flowers were worked at careful equidistance. It had been the tenant of her mother's workbasket all the preceding summer.

"My, she does beautiful work!" Mrs. Reuter fingered the dress tenderly. "Did you have some Nesselrode?" She nodded to Hester and left her.

"That's him," Clara whispered, at Hester's elbow.

"Where?"

"By the window," said Clara. She left Hester and went over to her mother.

Looking, Hester saw a man somewhat under middle height standing near Mrs. Enke. Against the Wagnerian proportions of the others, he appeared unobtrusive but not negligible, as if their fleshy tide might flow past but not engulf him. There was something about his pleasant, even-featured face that was as firm and self-contained as a nut. He crossed the room to speak to Mrs. Braggiotti, whose head and neck made a pretty arc as she inclined upward toward him, her circlet of crystal beads shining in the afternoon sun. Clara pranced over to Hester again. "Guess what!" she said. "George is going to take you and me and Mama for a soda!"

"Maybe I better not go."

"Oh, sure. It's just to a drugstore, silly. He *owns* it — a nice one, not like the one downstairs. Over on Madison Avenue. You needn't even tell your family you're going. I'll lend you a coat, and we can take turns on my skates. Come *on!*"

They walked the few blocks over to Madison Avenue, George and Mrs. Braggiotti far ahead, linked as sedately as any married couple. Combined with the cold thrill of the brilliant afternoon Hester felt the lovely unease of wearing someone else's clothes. As they walked, they could glimpse the frozen brown fronds of the park between the tall buildings, on which the hard, white winter sun struck, audible as a gong.

Set discreetly into the limestone corner of a block of private houses, Sunday-quiet behind their fretworks of iron, the ruby urns of the Town Pharmacy sent out a message of mystery and warmth. George unlocked the door and let them in to the aromatic smells of the pharmacopoeia and vanilla. Rising from the long expanse of tiled floor, the glass shelves, serried with pomades and panaceas, looked housewifely and knowledgeable, as if filled with the lore of the ages. Clara rushed to the small marble counter near the door and balanced on one of the high, curved metal chairs.

"A sundae, George, with everything."

"I don't open until four, Madam," he said, sliding off his coat and standing revealed in his suspenders and full, white shirtsleeves before he slipped on an alpaca jacket. Hester thought that he looked very intimate, but Mrs. Braggiotti, sitting formally on another chair, one pale-blue heel hooked over the rung, seemed not to notice. She refused a sundae, saying, "Oh, no, George, thanks. You know Mama's dinners!," in her high, untimbred voice.

After the sundaes, Hester and Clara went outside. Clara put on her skates and, promising not to take too long a turn, went grinding down the empty asphalt, rounded a corner, and was gone. Hester grew chilly waiting, and the sundae was cold inside her. Tiptoeing back around the half-open door into the store, she crouched down on a wooden box behind the marble counter and fingered the levers that controlled the soda water and syrups. Warm and hemmed in, she felt that it would be good to spend one's life in this shadowy store, away from the airless routine of an apartment but suspended a step above the rough street — like being on a little island, with faucets for running water and a bathroom at the back. There was a movement at the darker end of the store.

"Etta!" George's voice said pleadingly. "Etta!"

Hester peered out cautiously. Mrs. Braggiotti, hatless now, was pressed back against the prescription counter, leaning away from George, who stood in front of her with his hands against her waist.

"No, George." She reached along the counter to her hat, but he caught at her hand. They looked awkward, as if they were about to begin dancing but were not sure of the steps.

"We're not young enough to go on like this," he said. "Courting, like a couple of kids." Mrs. Braggiotti looked back at him woodenly, between her brows the same perplexed groove that she wore at the piano. She looked stilted, like an actress unsure of her lines. "Sometimes I think that's all you want," George said. "Someone hanging around." His voice sank.

Mrs. Braggiotti worked her blue shoe on the tiled floor, like a child enduring a familiar reproof.

"Why do you always" — he gripped her shoulders — "do you always . . ." He dropped his hands. "You can't go on forever being the pretty Reuter girl. Not even you."

She reached along the counter again, her rings chipping

the light, her hand smoothing the hat expertly, assuredly. The hand wandered to the nape of her neck, patting the smooth hair, outlining, reassuring. He seized her with a kiss that grew, his face deep red, his hand kneading around and around on her back, one dark, tailored thigh thrust forward against the watery design of her dress. Inside Hester, a buried pleasure turned over, and vague, ill-gotten rumors and confirmations chased in her head.

Mrs. Braggiotti pushed George away sharply. "My shoe! Oh, you've got dirt all over my shoe!" She bent down to brush it, real distress on her face.

"What is it you *do* want, Etta?"

Mrs. Braggiotti tilted her face up at him, her eyes clear, her forehead unfurrowed. "Why, I don't want anything, George," she said, in the same tone with which she had refused the sundae.

Hester crept out of her niche and slid carefully around the door. Across the street, the other limestone houses were still there, withdrawn, giving out none of their meaning. Behind her, the dim island of the store no longer drew her with its promise of suspension, of retreat. Looking down at her hands, she thought suddenly that they were a good color; it was the lavender voile that was wrong. She wavered against the blind hush of the street, wishing it full of people she could jostle, buffet, and embrace. Down the block she saw Clara coming back, her skates clashing and chiming. She drew a long breath and stepped further out into the seminal sunlight.

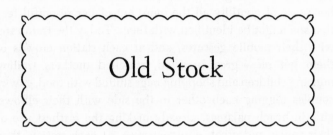

Old Stock

THE train creaked through the soft, heat-promising morning like an elderly, ambulatory sofa. Nosing along, it pushed its corridor of paper-spattered floors and old plush seats through towns whose names — Crystal Run, Mamakating — were as soft as the morning, and whose dusty little central hearts — all livery stable, freight depot, and yard buildings with bricked-up windows and faded sides that said "Purina Chows" — were as down-at-the-heel as the train that strung them together.

Hester, feeling the rocking stir of the journey between her thighs, hanging her head out of the window with her face snubbed against the hot breeze, tried to seize and fix each picture as it passed. At fifteen, everything she watched and heard seemed like a footprint on the trail of some eventuality she rode to meet, which never resolved but filled her world with a verve of waiting.

Opposite her, her mother sat with the shuttered, conscious look she always assumed in public places. Today there was that added look Hester also knew well, that prim display of **extra** restraint her mother always wore in the presence of other Jews whose grosser features, voices, manners offended her sense of gentility all the more out of her resentful fear that she might be identified with them. Today the train rang with their mobile gestures, and at each station crowds of them got off — great-breasted, starched mothers trailing mincing children and shopping bags stuffed with food, gawky couples digging each other in the side with their elbows, girls in beach pajamas, already making the farthest use of their smiles and great, effulgent eyes. At each station, they were met by the battered Fords and wagons that serviced the farms which would accommodate them, where for a week or two they would litter the tight Catskill towns with their swooping gaiety and their weary, rapacious hope.

"Wild!" said Mrs. Elkin, sotto voce, pursing her mouth and tucking her chin in her neck. "Your hair and that getup! Always so wild." Hester, injured, understood that the indictment was as much for the rest of the train as for herself. Each summer for the past three years, ever since Mr. Elkin's business had been doing poorly and the family had been unable to afford the summer rental in Westchester, Mrs. Elkin had resisted the idea of Old Corner Farm, and each year she had given in, for they were still of a status which made it unthinkable that they would not leave New York for some part of the season. This year and last, they had not been able to manage it until September, with its lowered rates, but it would have been a confession of defeat for Mr. Elkin had he not been able to say during the week to casual business acquaintances, "Family's up in the country. I go up weekends." Once at the farm — although the guests there were of a somewhat different class from the people in this train, most of them arriving in their own cars and one or two with nursegirls for the children — Mrs. Elkin would hold herself aloof at first, bending over her embroidery hoop on the veranda, receiving the complimentary "What gorgeous work you do!" with a *moue* of distaste for the flamboyant word that was a hallmark of what she hated in her own race, politely refusing proffered rides to the village, finally settling the delicate choice of summer intimacy on some cowed spinster or recessive widow whom life had dampened to the necessary refinement. For Mrs. Elkin walked through the world swinging the twangy words "refined," "refinement," like a purifying censer before her.

Hester, roused momentarily from her dream of the towns, looked idly across at her mother's neat navy-and-white version of the late-summer uniform of the unadventurous and the well bred. Under any hat, in any setting, her mother always looked enviably right, and her face, purged of those youthful exoticisms it once might well have had, had at last attained a welcomed anonymity, so that now it was like a medallion whose blurred handsomeness bore no denomination other than the patent, accessible one of "lady." Recently, Hester had begun to doubt the very gentility of her mother's exorcistic term itself, but she was still afraid to say so, to put a finger on this one of the many ambiguities that confronted her on every side. For nowadays it seemed to her that she was like someone forming a piece of crude statuary which had to be reshaped each day — that it was not her own character which was being formed but that she was putting together, from whatever clues people would let her have, the shifty, elusive character of the world.

"Summitville!" the conductor called, poking his head into the car.

Hester and her mother got off the train with a crowd of others. Their feet crunched in the cinders of the path. The shabby snake of the train moved forward through its rut in the checkerboard hills. Several men who had been leaning on battered Chevvies ran forward, hawking persistently, but Mrs. Elkin shook her head. "There's Mr. Smith!" She waved daintily at an old man standing beside a truck. They were repeat visitors. They were being met.

Mrs. Elkin climbed into the high seat and sat tight-elbowed between Mr. Smith and Hester, denying the dusty indignity of the truck. The Smiths, people with hard faces the color of snuff, made no concession to boarders other than clean lodging and massive food. Mr. Smith, whose conversation and clothing were equally gnarled, drove silently on. At the first sight of him, of old Mr. Smith, with his drooping scythe of mustache, Hester, in one jolt, had remembered everything from the summers before.

The farm they travelled toward lay in a valley off the road from Kerhonkson to Accord. The house, of weather-beaten stone, was low and thick, like a blockhouse still retreating suspiciously behind a stockade long since gone; upstairs, beaverboard had partitioned it into many molasses-tinted rooms. In front of it would be the covered well, where the summer people made a ceremony of their dilettante thirst, the children forever sawing on the pulley, the grown-ups smacking their lips over the tonic water not drawn from pipes. Mornings, after breakfast, the city children gravitated to the barn with the indecipherable date over its lintel and stood silent watching the cows, hearing their soft droppings, smelling the fecund smell that was like the perspiration the earth made in moving. Afterward, Hester, usually alone, followed the path down to the point where the brown waters of Schoharie Creek, which featherstitched the countryside for miles, ran, darkly overhung, across a great fan of ledges holding in their center one deep, minnow-flecked pool, like a large hazel eye.

"There's Miss Onderdonk's!" Hester said suddenly. They were passing a small, square house that still preserved the printlike, economical look of order of old red brick houses, although its once-white window frames were weathered and shutterless, and berry bushes, advancing from the great thorny bower of them at the back, scraggled at the first-floor windows and scratched at the three stone steps that brinked the rough-cut patch of lawn. A collie, red-gold and white, lay on the top step. "There's Margaret!" she added. "Oh, let's go see them after lunch!"

A minute before, if asked, Hester could not have told the name of the dog, but now she remembered everything: Miss Onderdonk, deaf as her two white cats, which she seemed to prize for their affliction (saying often how it was related in some way to their blue eyes and stainless fur), and Miss Onderdonk's parlor, with a peculiar, sooty darkness in its air that Hester had never seen anywhere else, as if shoe blacking had been mixed with it, or as if the only sources of light in it were the luminous reflections from the horse-hair chairs. Two portraits faced you as you entered from the bare, poor wood of the kitchen; in fact, you had only to turn on your heel from the splintered drainboard or the match-cluttered oilstove to see them — Miss Onderdonk's "great-greats" — staring nastily from their unlashed eyes, their pale faces and hands emerging from their needle-fine ruffles. The left one, the man, with a face so wide and full it must surely have been redder in life, kept his sneer directly on you, but the woman, her long chin resting in the ruffle, one forefinger and thumb pinching at the lush green velvet of her dress as if to draw it away, stared past you into the kitchen, at the bare drainboard and the broken-paned window above it.

Last year, Hester had spent much of her time "helping Miss Onderdonk," partly because there was no one her own age at the farm with whom to while away the long afternoons, partly because Miss Onderdonk's tasks were so different from anyone else's, since she lived, as she said, "offen the land." Miss Onderdonk was one of those deaf persons who do not chatter; her remarks hung singly, like aphorisms, in Hester's mind. "All white cats are deaf." "Sugar, salt, lard — bacon, flour, tea. The rest is offen the land." The articles thus enumerated lodged firmly in Hester's memory, shaped like the canisters so marked that contained the only groceries Miss Onderdonk seemed to have. Most of the time, when Hester appeared, Miss Onderdonk did not spare a greeting but drew her by an ignoring silence into the task at hand — setting out pans of berries to ferment in the hot sun, culling the warty carrots and spotted tomatoes from her dry garden. Once, when she and Hester were picking blackberries from bushes so laden that, turning slowly, they could pick a quart in one spot, Hester, plucking a fat berry, had also plucked a bee on its other side.

"Best go home. Best go home and mud it," Miss Onderdonk had said, and had turned back to the tinny plop of berries in her greedy pail. She had not offered mud. Hester, returning the next day, had not even felt resentment, for there was something about Miss Onderdonk, even if one did not quite like her, that compelled. As she worked at her endless ministrations to herself in her faded kitchen and garden, she was just like any other old maid, city or country, whose cottony hair was prigged tight from nightly crimpings never brushed free, whose figure, boarded up in an arid dress, made Hester gratefully, uneasily aware of her own body, fresh and moist. But when Miss Onderdonk stepped into her parlor, when she sat with her hands at rest on the carved knurls of the rocker or, standing near the open calf-bound book that chronicled the Onderdonk descent from De Witt Clinton, clasped her hands before her on some invisible pommel — then her role changed. When she stepped into her parlor, Miss Onderdonk swelled.

"How *is* Miss Onderdonk, Mr. Smith?" Mrs. Elkin asked lightly.

"The same." Mr. Smith kept his eyes on the road.

They turned in to the narrow dirt road that led off the highway down to the farm. Hester recognized a familiar curve in the sweep of surrounding hills, patch-quilted with crops. "There are hardly any white patches this year," she said.

Mr. Smith flicked a look at her, almost as if she had said something sensible. "People don't eat much buckwheat any more," he said, and brought the truck to a bumpy stop in front of the covered well.

Hester and her mother ran the gantlet of interested glances on the porch and went up to their room. The room had a mail-order austerity, with nothing in it that was not neutralized for the transient except the dim cross-stitch doily on the dresser. Hester was glad to see their clothing shut away in the tar-paper wardrobe, sorry to see their toilet articles, the beginning of clutter, ranged on the dresser. This was the most exciting moment of all, before the room settled down with your own coloration, before the people you would get to know were explored.

"I saw that Mrs. Garfunkel on the porch," she said.

Her mother said "Yes" as if she had pins in her mouth, and went on putting things in drawers.

Mrs. Garfunkel was one of the ones who said "gorgeous"; it was perhaps her favorite word. A young matron with reddish hair, chunky, snub features, and skin tawnied over with freckles, she had the look of a Teddy bear fresh from the shop. Up here, she dressed very quietly, with an absence of heels and floppy sunwear that, with her pug features, might have satisfied certain requirements in Mrs. Elkin's category of refinement. Neither did she talk with her hands, touch your clothing with them, or openly give the prices of things. But it was with her eyes that she estimated, with her tongue that she preened, and it was not long before you discovered that her admiring comment on some detail of your equipment was really only a springboard for the description of one or the other of her own incomparable possessions. Her satisfaction in these rested in their being not only the best but the best acquired for the least: the furs bought in August, the West Indian nursegirl who would work a year or so before realizing that the passage money Mrs. Garfunkel had advanced was more than underwritten by her inequitable salary, the compliant, self-effacing Mr. Garfunkel, who would probably go on working forever without realizing anything — even the languid, six-year-old Arline, who was so exactly suitable that she might have been acquired, after the canniest negotiation, from someone in that line to whom Mrs. Garfunkel had had a card of introduction. Perhaps, Hester thought now, her mother could better have borne Mrs. Garfunkel and her bargains if all of them had not been so successful.

When Hester and her mother, freshly washed and diffidently late, entered the dining room for dinner, which was in the middle of the day here, Mrs. Garfunkel hailed them, called them over to her table, pressed them to sit there, and introduced them to the others already seated. "Mrs. Elkin's an old-timer, like Mel and me. Meet Mr. and Mrs. Brod, and Mr. Brod's mother. And my brother Wally, Mrs. Elkin and daughter. What's your name again, dear?" She paid no heed to Hester's muttered response but dug her arm affectionately against the side of the rickety young man with slick hair who sat next to her, doggedly accumulating food on his plate. "Wally ran up here to get away from half the girls in Brooklyn."

The young man gave her a look of brotherly distaste. "Couldn't have come to a better place," he said, and returned to his plate. Great platters of sliced beefsteak tomatoes and fricasseed chicken were passed, nubs of Country Gentleman corn were snatched and snatched again; the table was one flashing activity of reaching arms, although there was much more food upon it than the few of them could possibly eat. This amplitude was what one came for, after all, and this was its high point, after which there would be nothing much to look forward to through the afternoon daze of heat but supper, which was good, though not like this.

Eating busily, Hester, from under the wing of her mother's monosyllabic chilliness, watched Mr. and Mrs. Brod. They were newly married, it developed, but this was not the honeymoon. The honeymoon, as almost every turn in the conversation indicated, had been in California; they were at the farm to visit old Mrs. Brod, a little leathery grandmother of a woman, dressed in a jaunty Roman-stripe jumper and wearing a ribbon tied around hair that had been bobbed and blued. The young Mrs. Brod had a sleepy melon face with a fat mouth, dark-red nails, and black hair cut Buster Brown. Mr. Brod, a bald young man in fawn-colored jacket and knickers, said almost nothing, but every so often he did an extraordinary thing. At intervals, his wife, talking busily, would extend her hand sidewise, palm upward, without even looking at him, and in one convulsive movement that seemed to start somewhere outside him and end at his extremities, as if he were the tip of a smartly cracked whip, a gold case would be miraculously there in his hand, and he would place a cigarette tenderly in her palm. A second but lesser convulsion produced a lighter for the negligently held cigarette. He did not smoke.

The two Mrs. Brods were discussing the dress worn by the younger, evidently a California purchase. "Right away, I said, 'This one I take!'" said the bride. "Definitely a knockout!"

"Vunt vash," said her mother-in-law, munching on an ear of corn.

The bride shrugged. "So I'll give to cleaners."

"Give to clean, give to ket." The mother put down her ear of corn, rolling it over reflectively.

"Don't have a cat, Ma."

Mrs. Brod the elder turned away momentarily from her plate. "Sah yull *buy* ah ket!" she said, and one lean brown arm whipped out and took another ear of corn.

The bride looked miffed, then put out the cigarette-seeking hand. Flex, flash from the solicitous Mr. Brod and the cigarette, lit, was between her lips, smoke curling from her scornful nostrils.

"Sweet, isn't it, the way he does that? And not a smoke for himself," said Mrs. Garfunkel in an aside to Hester's mother. "You better watch out, Syl," she called across the table to the bride. "He forgets to do that, then the honeymoon is over."

Mrs. Elkin smiled, a little rigid but perfectly cordial, unless you knew the signs, and stood up, reaching around for her big knitting bag, which was hung on the back of her chair. "Come, dear," she said to Hester, in accents at which no purist could cavil. "Suppose you and I go out on the porch."

On the empty porch, Mrs. Elkin selected a chair far down at the end. "Those people!" she said, and blew her breath sharply between set teeth. "I told your father this place was getting rundown."

"Sah yull *buy* ah ket," said Hester dreamily, and chuckled. It was the illogic of the remark that charmed.

"Must you *imitate?*" said her mother.

"But it's funny, Mother."

"Oh, you're just like your father. Absolutely without discrimination."

Hester found nothing to answer. "I think I'll walk down to the creek," she said.

"Take a towel."

Hester ran upstairs. Suddenly it was urgent that she get down to the creek alone, before the others, digestion accomplished, went there to bathe. Upstairs, she shed her clothes swiftly and crammed herself into last year's bathing suit — tight and faded, but it would not matter here. She ran downstairs, crossed the porch without looking at her mother, and ran across the lawn into the safety of the path, which had a wall of weeds on either side. Once there, she walked on, slow and happy. The wire tangle of weeds was alive with stalks and pods and beadlets of bright green whose shapes she knew well but could not, need not, name. Above all, it was the same.

She pushed through the bushes that fringed the creek. It, too, was the same. In the past year, it must have gone through all the calendar changes. She imagined each of them — the freeze, the thaw, the spring running, like conventionalized paper pictures torn off one by one — but they were as unreal as the imagined private dishabille of a friend. Even the bushes that ran for miles along its edge were at the same stage of their bloom, their small, cone-shaped orange flowers dotted along the leaves for as far as she could see. The people around the farm called them "scarlet runners," although their flowers were as orange as a color could be.

She trod carefully across the slippery ledges out to the wide, flat slab that rose in the middle of the stream, and stretched out on her stomach on its broad, moss-slimed back. She lay there for a long time looking into the eye of the pool. One need not have an appointment with minnows, she thought. They are always the same, too.

At a crackling sound in the brush, she looked up. Mrs. Garfunkel's head appeared above the greenery, which ended in a ruff at her neck, like the painted backdrops behind which people pose at amusement parks. "Your mother says to tell you she's gone on down to Miss Onderdonk's." She waited while Hester picked her way back to shore. Until Hester gained the high weeds of the path, she felt the Teddy-bear eyes watching idly, calculating and squint.

In her room once more, Hester changed to a paper-dry cotton dress, then hurried out again, down the dirt road this time, and onto the state highway, slowing down only when she was in sight of Miss Onderdonk's house, and saw her mother and Miss Onderdonk sitting facing one another, one on each of the two butterfly-winged wooden benches built on the top step at either side of the door, forming the only porch there was.

"Why that dress?" asked her mother, with fair reason, for it was Hester's best. "You remember Hester, Miss Onderdonk?" she added.

Miss Onderdonk looked briefly at Hester with her watery, time-eclipsing stare. There was no indication that she knew Hester's name, or ever had. One of the white cats lay resiliently on her lap, with the warning look of toleration common to cats when held. Miss Onderdonk, like the creek, might have lived suspended from last September to this, untouched by the flowing year, every crimp in her hair the same. And the parlor? It would have to be seen, for certain.

Hester sat down quietly next to her mother, whose sewing went on and on, a mild substitute for conversation. For a while, Hester watched the long, important-looking shadows that encroached upon the hills, like enigmas stated every afternoon but never fully solved. Then she leaned carefully toward Miss Onderdonk. "May I go see your parlor?" she asked.

Miss Onderdonk gave no sign that she had heard. It might have been merely the uncanny luck of the partly deaf that prompted her remark. "People come by here this morning," she said. "From down to your place. Walk right into the parlor, no by-your-leave. Want to buy my antiques!"

Mrs. Elkin, needle uplifted, shook her head, commiserating, gave a quick, consolatory mew of understanding, and plunged the needle into the next stitch.

"Two women — and a man all ninnied out for town," said Miss Onderdonk. "Old woman had doctored hair. Grape-colored! Hollers at me as if I'm the foreign one. Picks up my Leather-Bound Onderdonk History!" Her explosive breath capitalized the words. The cat, squirting suddenly from her twitching hand, settled itself, an aggrieved white tippet, at a safe distance on the lawn. " 'Put that down,' I said," said Miss Onderdonk, her eyes as narrow as the cat's. " 'I don't have no antiques,' I said. 'These here are my belongings.' "

Mrs. Elkin put down her sewing. Her broad hands, with the silver-and-gold thimble on one middle finger, moved uncertainly, unlike Miss Onderdonk's hands, which were pressed flat, in triumph, on her faded, flour-sack lap.

"I told Elizabeth Smith," Miss Onderdonk said. "I told her she'd rue the day she ever started taking in Jews."

The short word soared in an arc across Hester's vision and hit the remembered, stereopticon picture of the parlor. The parlor sank and disappeared, a view in an album snapped shut. Now her stare was for her mother's face, which was pink but inconclusive.

Mrs. Elkin, raising her brows, made a helpless face at Hester, as if to say, "After all, the vagaries of the deaf . . ." She permitted herself a minimal shrug, even a slight spreading of palms. Under Hester's stare, she lowered her eyes and turned toward Miss Onderdonk again.

"I thought you knew, Miss Onderdonk," said her mother. "I thought you knew that we were — Hebrews." The word, the ultimate refinement, slid out of her mother's soft voice as if it were on runners.

"Eh?" said Miss Onderdonk.

Say it, Hester prayed. She had never before felt the sensation of prayer. Please say it, Mother. *Say "Jew."* She heard the word in her own mind, double-voiced, like the ram's horn at Yom Kippur, with an ugly present bray but with a long, urgent echo as time-spanning as Roland's horn.

Her mother leaned forward. Perhaps she had heard it, too — the echo. "But we are Jewish," she said in a stronger voice. "Mr. Elkin and I are Jewish."

Miss Onderdonk shook her head, with the smirk of one who knew better. "Never seen the Mister. The girl here has the look, maybe. But not you."

"But — " Mrs. Elkin, her lower lip caught by her teeth, made a sound like a stifled, chiding sigh. "Oh, yes," she said, and nodded, smiling, as if she had been caught out in a fault.

"Does you credit," said Miss Onderdonk. "Don't say it don't. Make your bed, lie on it. Don't have to pretend with me, though."

With another baffled sigh, Mrs. Elkin gave up, flumping her hands down on her sewing. She was pinker, not with anger but, somehow, as if she had been cajoled.

"Had your reasons, maybe." Miss Onderdonk tittered, high and henlike. "Ain't no Jew, though. Good blood shows, any day."

Hester stood up. "We're in a book at home, too," she said loudly. " 'The History of the Jews of Richmond, 1769–1917.' " Then she turned her back on Miss Onderdonk, who might or might not have heard, on her mother, who had, and stomped down the steps.

At the foot of the lawn, she stopped behind a bush that hid her from the steps, feeling sick and let-down. She had somehow used Miss Onderdonk's language. She hadn't said what she meant at all. She heard her father's words, amused and sad, as she had heard them once, over her shoulder, when he had come upon her poring over the red-bound book, counting up the references to her grandfather. "That Herbert Ezekiel's book?" He had looked over her shoulder, twirling the gold cigar-clipper on his watch chain. "Well, guess it won't hurt the sons of Moses any if they want to tally up some newer ancestors now and then."

Miss Onderdonk's voice, with its little, cut-off chicken

laugh, travelled down to her from the steps. "Can't say it didn't cross my mind, though, that the girl does have the look."

Hester went out onto the highway and walked quickly back to the farmhouse. Skirting the porch, she tiptoed around to one side, over to an old fringed hammock slung between two trees whose broad bottom fronds almost hid it. She swung herself into it, covered herself over with the side flaps, and held herself stiff until the hammock was almost motionless.

Mrs. Garfunkel and Arline could be heard on the porch, evidently alone, for now and then Mrs. Garfunkel made óne of the fretful, absent remarks mothers make to children when no one else is around. Arline had some kind of wooden toy that rumbled back and forth across the porch. Now and then, a bell on it went "ping."

After a while, someone came along the path and up on the porch. Hester lay still, the hammock fringe tickling her face. "Almost time for supper," she heard Mrs. Garfunkel say.

"Yes," said her mother's voice. "Did Hester come back this way?"

"I was laying down for a while. Arline, dear, did you see Hester?"

"No, Mummy." "Ping, ping" went Arline's voice.

" 'Mummy'!" said Mrs. Garfunkel. "That's that school she goes to — you know the Kemp-Willard School, on Eighty-sixth?"

"Oh, yes," said Mrs. Elkin. "Quite good, I've heard."

"Good!" Mrs. Garfunkel sighed, on a sleek note of outrage. "What they soak you, they ought to be."

Arline's toy rumbled across the porch again and was still.

"She'll come back when she's hungry, I suppose," said Mrs. Elkin. "There was a rather unfortunate little — incident, down the road."

"Shush, Arline. You don't say?"

Chairs scraped confidentially closer. Mrs. Elkin's voice dropped to the low, *gemütlich* whisper reserved for obstetrics, cancer, and the peculations of servant girls. Once or twice, the whisper, flurrying higher, shook out a gaily audible phrase. "Absolutely wouldn't believe — " "Can you imagine anything so silly?" Then, in her normal voice, "Of course, she's part deaf, and probably a little crazy from being alone so much."

"Scratch any of them and you're sure to find it," said Mrs. Garfunkel.

"Ah, well," said Mrs. Elkin. "But it certainly was funny," she added, in a voice velveted over now with a certain savor of reminiscence, "the way she kept *insisting*."

"Uh-huh," said Mrs. Garfunkel rather flatly. "Yeah. Sure."

Someone came out on the back porch and vigorously swung the big bell that meant supper in fifteen minutes.

"Care for a little drive in the Buick after supper?" asked Mrs. Garfunkel.

"Why — why, yes," said Mrs. Elkin, her tones warmer now with the generosity of one whose equipment went beyond the realm of bargains. "Why, I think that would be very nice."

"Any time," said Mrs. Garfunkel. "Any time you want stamps or anything. Thought you might enjoy a little ride. Not having the use of a car."

The chairs scraped back, the screen door creaked, and the two voices, linked in their sudden, dubious rapprochement, went inside. The scuffling toy followed them.

Hester rolled herself out of the hammock and stood up. She looked for comfort at the reasonable hills, whose pat‑ tern changed only according to what people ate; at the path, down which there was nothing more ambiguous than the hazel-eyed water or the flower that should be scarlet but was orange. While she had been in the hammock, the dusk had covered them over. It had settled over everything with its rapt, misleading veil.

She walked around to the foot of the front steps. A thin, emery edge of autumn was in the air now. Inside, they must all be at supper; no one else had come by. When she walked into the dining room, they would all lift their heads for a moment, the way they always did when someone walked in late, all of them regarding her for just a minute with their equivocal adult eyes. Something would rise from them all like a warning odor, confusing and corrupt, and she knew now what it was. Miss Onderdonk sat at their table, too. Wherever any of them sat publicly at table, Miss Onder- donk sat at his side. Only, some of them set a place for her and some of them did not.

{ The Middle Drawer }

The drawer was always kept locked. In a household where the tangled rubbish of existence had collected on surfaces like a scurf, which was forever being cleared away by her mother and the maid, then by her mother, and, finally, hardly at all, it had been a permanent cell — rather like, Hester thought wryly, the gene that is carried over from one generation to the other. Now, holding the small, square, indelibly known key in her hand, she shrank before it, reluctant to perform the blasphemy that the living must inevitably perpetrate on the possessions of the dead. There were no revelations to be expected when she opened the drawer, only the painful reiteration of her mother's personality and the power it had held over her own, which would rise — an emanation, a mist, that she herself had long since shredded away, parted, and escaped.

She repeated to herself, like an incantation, "I am married. I have a child of my own, a home of my own five hundred miles away. I have not even lived in this house — my parents' house — for over seven years." Stepping back, she sat on the bed where her mother had died the week before, slowly, from cancer, where Hester had held the large, long-fingered, competent hand for a whole night, watching the asphyxiating action of the fluid mounting in the lungs until it had extinguished the breath. She sat facing the drawer.

It had taken her all her own lifetime to get to know its full contents, starting from the first glimpses, when she was just able to lean her chin on the side and have her hand pushed away from the packets and japanned boxes, to the last weeks, when she had made a careful show of not noticing while she got out the necessary bankbooks and safe-deposit keys. Many times during her childhood, when she had lain blandly ill herself, elevated to the honor of the parental bed while she suffered from the "autointoxication" that must have been 1918's euphemism for plain piggishness, the drawer had been opened. Then she had been allowed to play with the two pairs of pearled opera glasses or the long string of graduated white china beads, each with its oval sides flushed like cheeks. Over these she had sometimes spent the whole afternoon, pencilling two eyes and a pursed mouth on each bead, until she had achieved an incredible string of minute, doll-like heads that made even her mother laugh.

Once while Hester was in collége, the drawer had been opened for the replacement of her grandmother's great sun-burst pin, which she had never before seen and which had been in pawn, and doggedly reclaimed over a long period by her mother. And for Hester's wedding her mother had taken out the delicate diamond chain — the "lavaliere" of the Gibson-girl era — that had been her father's wedding gift to her mother, and the ugly, expensive bar pin that had been his gift to his wife on the birth of her son. Hester had never before seen either of them, for the fashion of wearing diamonds indiscriminately had never been her mother's, who was contemptuous of other women's display, although she might spend minutes in front of the mirror debating a choice between two relatively gimcrack pieces of costume jewelry. Hester had never known why this was until recently, when the separation of the last few years had relaxed the tension between her mother and herself — not enough to prevent explosions when they met but enough for her to see obscurely, the long motivations of her mother's life. In the European sense, family jewelry was Property, and with all her faultless English and New World poise, her mother had never exorcised her European core.

In the back of the middle drawer, there was a small square of brown-toned photograph that had never escaped into the large, ramshackle portfolio of family pictures kept in the drawer of the old break-front bookcase, open to any hand. Seated on a bench, Hedwig Licht, aged two, brows knitted under ragged hair, stared mournfully into the camera with the huge, heavy-lidded eyes that had continued to brood in her face as a woman, the eyes that she had transmitted to Hester, along with the high cheekbones that she had deplored. Fat, wrinkled stockings were bowed into arcs that almost met at the high-stretched boots, which did not touch the floor; to hold up the stockings, strips of calico matching the dumpy little dress were bound around the knees.

Long ago, Hester, in her teens, staring tenaciously into the drawer under her mother's impatient glance, had found the little square and exclaimed over it, and her mother, snatching it away from her, had muttered, "If that isn't Dutchy!" But she had looked at it long and ruefully before she had pushed it back into a corner. Hester had added the picture to the legend of her mother's childhood built up from the bitter little anecdotes that her mother had let drop casually over the years.

She saw the small Hedwig, as clearly as if it had been herself, haunting the stiff rooms of the house in the townlet of Oberelsbach, motherless since birth and almost immediately stepmothered by a woman who had been unloving, if not unkind, and had soon borne the stern, *Haustyrann* father a son. The small figure she saw had no connection with the all-powerful figure of her mother but, rather, seemed akin to the legion of lonely children who were a constant motif in the literature that had been her own drug — the Sara Crewes and Little Dorrits, all those children who inhabited the familiar terror-struck dark that crouched under the lash of the adult. She saw Hedwig receiving from her dead mother's mother — the Grandmother Rosenberg, warm and loving but, alas, too far away to be of help — the beautiful, satin-incrusted bisque doll, and she saw the bad stepmother taking it away from Hedwig and putting it in the drawing room, because "it is too beautiful for a child to play with." She saw all this as if it had happened to her and she had never forgotten.

Years later, when this woman, Hester's step-grandmother, had come to the United States in the long train of refugees from Hitler, her mother had urged the grown Hester to visit her, and she had refused, knowing her own childishness but feeling the resentment rise in her as if she were six, saying,

"I won't go. She wouldn't let you have your doll." Her mother had smiled at her sadly and had shrugged her shoulders resignedly. "You wouldn't say that if you could see her. She's an old woman. She has no teeth." Looking at her mother, Hester had wondered what her feeings were after forty years, but her mother, private as always in her emotions, had given no sign.

There had been no sign for Hester — never an open demonstration of love or an appeal — until the telephone call of a few months before, when she had heard her mother say quietly, over the distance, "I think you'd better come," and she had turned away from the phone saying bitterly, almost in awe, "If she *asks me* to come, she must be dying!"

Turning the key over in her hand, Hester looked back at the composite figure of her mother — that far-off figure of the legendary child, the nearer object of her own dependence, love, and hate — looked at it from behind the safe, dry wall of her own "American" education. We are told, she thought, that people who do not experience love in their earliest years cannot open up; they cannot give it to others; but by the time we have learned this from books or dredged it out of reminiscence, they have long since left upon us their chill, irremediable stain.

If Hester searched in her memory for moments of animal maternal warmth, like those she self-consciously gave her own child (as if her own childhood prodded her from behind), she thought always of the blue-shot twilight of one New York evening, the winter she was eight, when she and her mother were returning from a shopping expedition, gay and united in the shared guilt of being late for supper. In her mind, now, their arrested figures stood like two silhouettes caught in the spotlight of time. They had paused under the brightly agitated bulbs of a movie-theatre marquee, behind them the broad, rose-red sign of a Happiness candy store. Her mother, suddenly leaning down to her, had encircled her with her arm and nuzzled her, saying almost anxiously, "We do have fun together, don't we?" Hester had stared back stolidly, almost suspiciously, into the looming, pleading eyes, but she had rested against the encircling arm, and warmth had trickled through her as from a closed wound reopening.

After this, her mother's part in the years that followed seemed blurred with the recriminations from which Hester had retreated ever farther, always seeking the remote corners of the household — the sofa-fortressed alcoves, the store closet, the servants' bathroom — always bearing her amulet, a book. It seemed to her now, wincing, that the barrier of her mother's dissatisfaction with her had risen imperceptibly, like a coral cliff built inexorably from the slow accretion of carelessly ejaculated criticisms that had grown into solid being in the heavy fullness of time. Meanwhile, her father's uncritical affection, his open caresses, had been steadiness under her feet after the shifting waters of her mother's personality, but he had been away from home on business for long periods, and when at home he, too, was increasingly a target for her mother's deep-burning rage against life. Adored member of a large family that was almost tribal in its affections and unity, he could not cope with this smoldering force and never tried to understand it, but the shield of his adulthood gave him a protection that Hester did not have. He stood on equal ground.

Hester's parents had met at Saratoga, at the races. So dissimilar were their backgrounds that it was improbable that they would ever have met elsewhere than in the somewhat easy social flux of a spa, although their brownstone homes in New York were not many blocks apart, his in the gentility of upper Madison Avenue, hers in the solid, Germanic comfort of Yorkville. By this time, Hedwig had been in America ten years.

All Hester knew of her mother's coming to America was that she had arrived when she was sixteen. Now that she knew how old her mother had been at death, knew the birth date so zealously guarded during a lifetime of evasion and so quickly exposed by the noncommittal nakedness of funeral routine, she realized that her mother must have arrived in 1900. She had come to the home of an aunt, a sister of her own dead mother. What family drama had preceded her coming, whose decision it had been, Hester did not know. Her mother's one reply to a direct question had been a shrugging "There was nothing for me there."

Hester had a vivid picture of her mother's arrival and first years in New York, although this was drawn from only two clues. Her great-aunt, remarking once on Hester's looks in the dispassionate way of near relations, had nodded over Hester's head to her mother. "She is dark, like the father, no? Not like you were." And Hester, with a naïve glance of surprise at her mother's sedate pompadour, had eagerly interposed, "What was she like, Tante?"

"*Ach,* when she came off the boat, *war sie hübsch!*" Tante had said, lapsing into German with unusual warmth, "Such a color! Pink and cream!"

"Yes, a real Bavarian *Mädchen*," said her mother with a trace of contempt. "Too pink for the fashion here. I guess they thought it wasn't real."

Another time, her mother had said, in one of her rare bursts of anecdote, "When I came, I brought enough linen and underclothing to supply two brides. At the convent school where I was sent, the nuns didn't teach you much besides embroidery, so I had plenty to bring, plenty. They were nice, though. Good, simple women. Kind. I remember I brought four dozen handkerchiefs, beautiful heavy linen that you don't get in America. But they were large, bigger than the size of a man's handkerchief over here, and the first time I unfolded one, everybody laughed, so I threw them away." She had sighed, perhaps for the linen. "And underdrawers! Long red flannel, and I had spent months embroidering them with yards of white eyelet work on the ruffles. I remember Tante's maid came in from the back yard quite angry and refused to hang them on the line any more. She said the other maids, from the houses around, teased her for belonging to a family who would wear things like that."

Until Hester was in her teens, her mother had always employed young German or Czech girls fresh from "the other side" — Teenies and Josies of long braided hair, broad cotton ankles and queer, blunt shoes, who had clacked deferentially to her mother in German and had gone off to marry their waiter's and baker's apprentices at just about the time they learned to wear silk stockings and "just as soon as you've taught them how to serve a dinner," returning regularly to show off their square, acrid babies. "Greenhorns!" her mother had always called them, a veil of something indefinable about her lips. But in the middle drawer there was a long rope of blond hair, sacrificed, like the handkerchiefs, but not wholly discarded.

There was no passport in the drawer. Perhaps it had been destroyed during the years of the first World War, when her mother, long since a citizen by virtue of her marriage, had felt the contemporary pressure to excise everything Teutonic. "If that nosy Mrs. Cahn asks you when I came over, just say I came over as a child," she had said to Hester. And how easy it had been to nettle her by pretending that one could discern a trace of accent in her speech! Once, when the family had teased her by affecting to hear an echo of "public" in her pronunciation of "public," Hester had come upon her, hours after, standing before a mirror, color and nose high, watching herself say, over and over again, "Public! Public!"

Was it this, thought Hester, her straining toward perfection, that made her so intolerant of me, almost as if she were castigating in her child the imperfections that were her own? "Big feet, big hands, like mine," her mother had grumbled. "Why? Why? When every woman in your father's family wears size one! But their nice, large ears — you must have *those!*" And dressing Hester for Sunday school she would withdraw a few feet to look at the finished product, saying slowly, with dreamy cruelty, "I don't know why I let you wear those white gloves. They make your hands look clumsy, just like a policeman's."

It was over books that the rift between Hester and her mother had become complete. To her mother, marrying into a family whose bookish traditions she had never ceased trying to undermine with the sneer of the practical, it was as if the stigmata of that tradition, appearing upon the girl, had forever made them alien to one another.

"Your eyes don't look like a girl's, they look like an old woman's! Reading! Forever reading!" she had stormed, chasing Hester from room to room, flushing her out of doors, and on one remote, terrible afternoon, whipping the book out of Hester's hand, she had leaned over her, glaring, and had torn the book in two.

Hester shivered now, remembering the cold sense of triumph that had welled up in her as she had faced her mother, rejoicing in the enormity of what her mother had done.

Her mother had faltered before her. "Do you want to be a dreamer all your life?" she had muttered.

Hester had been unable to think of anything to say for a moment. Then she had stuttered, "All you think of in life is money!," and had made her grand exit. But huddling miserably in her room afterward she had known even then that it was not as simple as that, that her mother, too, was whipped and driven by some ungovernable dream she could not express, which had left her, like the book, torn in two.

Was it this, perhaps, that had sent her across an ocean, that had impelled her to perfect her dress and manner, and to reject the humdrum suitors of her aunt's circle for a Virginia bachelor twenty-two years older than herself? Had she, perhaps, married him not only for his money and his seasoned male charm but also for his standards and traditions, against which her railings had been a confession of envy and defeat?

So Hester and her mother had continued to pit their implacable difference against each other in a struggle that was complicated out of all reason by their undeniable likeness — each pursuing in her own orbit the warmth that had been denied. Gauche and surly as Hester was in her mother's presence, away from it she had striven successfully for the very falsities of standard that she despised in her mother, and it was her misery that she was forever impelled to earn her mother's approval at the expense of her own. Always, she knew now, there had been the lurking, buried wish that someday she would find the final barb, the homing shaft, that would maim her mother once and for all, as she felt herself to have been maimed.

A few months before, the barb had been placed in her hand. In answer to the telephone call, she had come to visit the family a short time after her mother's sudden operation for cancer of the breast. She had found her father and brother in an anguish of helplessness, fear, and male distaste at the thought of the illness, and her mother a prima donna of fortitude, moving unbowed toward the unspoken idea of her death but with the signs on her face of a pitiful tension that went beyond the disease. She had taken to using separate utensils and to sleeping alone, although the medical opinion that cancer was not transferable by contact was well known to her. It was clear that she was suffering from a horror of what had been done to her and from a fear of the revulsion of others. It was clear to Hester, also, that her father and brother had such a revulsion and had not been wholly successful in concealing it.

One night she and her mother had been together in her mother's bedroom. Hester, in a shabby housegown, stretched out on the bed luxuriously, thinking of how there was always a certain equivocal ease, a letting down of pretense, an illusory return to the irresponsibility of childhood, in the house of one's birth. Her mother, back turned, had been standing unnecessarily long at the bureau, fumbling with the articles upon it. She turned slowly.

"They've been giving me X-ray twice a week," she said, not looking at Hester, "to stop any involvement of the glands."

"Oh," said Hester, carefully smoothing down a wrinkle on the bedspread. "It's very wise to have that done."

Suddenly, her mother had put out her hand in a gesture almost of appeal. Half in a whisper, she asked, "Would you like to see it? No one has seen it since I left the hospital."

"Yes," Hester said, keeping her tone cool, even, full only of polite interest. "I'd like very much to see it." Frozen there on the bed, she had reverted to childhood in reality, remembering, as if they had all been crammed into one slot in time, the thousands of incidents when she had been the one to stand before her mother, vulnerable and bare, helplessly awaiting the cruel exactitude of her displeasure. "I know how she feels as if I were standing there myself," thought Hester. "How well she taught me to know!"

Slowly her mother undid her housegown and bared her breast. She stood there for a long moment, on her face the looming, pleading look of twenty years before, the look it had once shown under the theatre marquee.

Hester half rose from the bed. There was a hurt in her own breast that she did not recognize. She spoke with difficulty.

"Why . . . it's a beautiful job, Mother," she said, distilling the carefully natural tone of her voice. "Neat as can be. I had no idea . . . I thought it would be ugly." With a step toward her mother, she looked, as if casually, at the dreadful neatness of the cicatrix, at the twisted, foreshortened tendon of the upper arm.

"I can't raise my arm yet," whispered her mother. "They had to cut deep. . . . Your father won't look at it."

In an eternity of slowness, Hester stretched out her hand. Trembling, she touched a tentative finger to her mother's chest, where the breast had been. Then, with rising sureness, with infinite delicacy, she drew her fingertips along the length of the scar in a light, affirmative caress, and they stood eye to eye for an immeasurable second, on equal ground at last.

In the cold, darkening room, Hester unclenched herself from remembrance. She was always vulnerable, Hester thought. As we all are. What she bequeathed me unwittingly, ironically, was fortitude — the fortitude of those who have had to live under the blow. But pity — that I found for myself.

She knew now that the tangents of her mother and herself would never have fully met, even if her mother had lived. Holding her mother's hand through the long night as she retreated over the border line of narcosis and coma into death, she had felt the giddy sense of conquering, the heady euphoria of being still alive, which comes to the watcher in the night. Nevertheless, she had known with sureness, even then, that she would go on all her life trying to "show" her mother, in an unsatisfied effort to earn her approval — and unconditional love.

As a child, she had slapped at her mother once in a frenzy of rebellion, and her mother, in reproof, had told her the tale of the peasant girl who had struck her mother and had later fallen ill and died and been buried in the village cemetery. When the mourners came to tend the mound, they found that the corpse's offending hand had grown out of the grave. They cut it off and reburied it, but when they came again in the morning, the hand had grown again. So, too, thought Hester, even though I might learn — have learned in some ways — to escape my mother's hand, all my life I will have to push it down; all my life my mother's hand will grow again out of the unquiet grave of the past.

It was her own life that was in the middle drawer. She was the person she was not only because of her mother but because, fifty-eight years before, in the little town of Oberelsbach, another woman, whose qualities she would never know, had died too soon. Death, she thought, absolves equally the bungler, the evildoer, the unloving, and the unloved — but never the living. In the end, the cicatrix that she had, in the smallest of ways, helped her mother to bear had eaten its way in and killed. The living carry, she thought, perhaps not one tangible wound but the burden of the innumerable small cicatrices imposed on us by our beginnings; we carry them with us always, and from these, from this agony, we are not absolved.

She turned the key and opened the drawer.